PLEASE, NO POLICE

MODERN MIDDLE EAST

LITERATURES IN TRANSLATION

SERIES

Aras Ören

Please, No Police

Translated from the Turkish
by
Teoman Sipahigil

Introduction by Akile Gürsoy Tezcan

Center for Middle Eastern Studies
University of Texas at Austin

Library of Congress Catalog Card Number: 92-075236

ISBN 0-292-76038-8

Printed in the United States of America

Cover Design: Diane Watts

Editor: Annes McCann-Baker

Table of Contents

Acknowledgments

The Center for Middle Eastern Studies at The University of Texas in Austin is proud to publish the twelfth volume in the Modern Middle East Literatures in Translation Series, a Series published in conjunction with the University of Texas Press. The Series presents fiction, memoirs, and literary criticism translated from Arabic, Hebrew, Persian, and Turkish.

We want to thank author Aras Ören for giving permission for an English translation of *Bitte nix Polizei*, his original version in Turkish of *Please, No Police*. We want to give special thanks to translator Teoman Sipahigil from the English Department at the University of Idaho for his meticulous and imaginative translation of the novella. And, for her lucid and informative Introduction, so necessary for placing *Please, No Police* in historical and literary context, we send our gratitude to Akile Gürsoy Tezcan at Marmara University in Istanbul.

Annes McCann-Baker

Editor

INTRODUCTION

The publication of *Please, No Police* by the Turkish writer Aras
Ören marks the English debut of what has been termed a new genre
in both Turkish and European literature. In the last thirty years,
more than 1,100 works have appeared, dealing with Turkish migrant
workers' experiences in Germany. Written mostly in Turkish, these
novels, short stories, and novellas have been seen as an emerging
sub-literature in Turkey.[1] Today, the work has assumed international cultural dimensions with the German critics' sudden and enthusiastic embracing of this literary production and giving it a label,
as *Gastarbeiterliteratur* (the literature of guest workers). Gisela Kraft
calls it "the most fascinating event in German history of the 20th
century."[2]

Before analyzing this new cross-cultural literature, however, it is
important to look at the economic and political history of the social
phenomenon which has produced it, the phenomenon known as
Turkish labor migration.

Labor migration is an important feature of post-war European
economic development and population composition. Since the 1950s,
the persistent excess labor demand in the more industrialized

---

[1]See bibliography containing more than 1,100 sources of works written in
Turkish, on Turkish experiences in Germany, mostly written in the last 30
years: *Über das Leben in Bitterland* (On Life in Bitter Land), by Wolfgang
Riemann, Otto Harrassowitz, Wiesbaden 1990.

[2]Gisela Kraft, "Türkische Literatur in deutscher Sprache: Übersetzernotizen
zu Beginn der achtziger Jahre," *Sprache im technischen Zeitalter*, no 82 (15
June 1982): 137.

economies of Western Europe has been matched by excess labor supply in the "less advanced" countries. It is estimated that today a total of about 15 million foreign workers and their families live in Europe. This figure is higher than the total population of most of Europe's countries taken individually. In other words, "every seventh man in Europe is a foreign worker."[3] Fifteen percent of all the foreign residents in Western Europe are estimated to be Turks, that is about 800,000 active workers and about three million Turkish residents. Out of this figure, about 600,000 active workers and about one-and-a-half million Turkish residents are estimated to be in Germany.

In the late 1950s, eager to find laborers for its expanding industry, Germany, like the other industrialized Western European countries, appealed to peripheral countries including Turkey to find needed individuals for its work force. For historic as well as geographic reasons, Germany received predominantly Turkish workers while France attracted Arab migrants and Holland received Asian workers.[4] In many Mediterranean countries with few occupational opportunities, external migration in the decades following the mid-fifties became a matter of governmental policy, frequently regulated by international bilateral agreements. The highly industrialized West European countries to which workers migrated exercised full employment policies and extended vocational training to the workers.

---

[3]John Berger and Jean Mohr, in Abadan-Unat, N. , "Identity Crisis of Turkish Migrants, First and Second Generation," in *Turkish Workers in Europe*, Indiana University Turkish Studies, 1985 (p. 3).
[4]Kazgan, G., *Prospects for Turkey's Accession to the Community*, (Report for SIAR: Social and Economic Research Inc.), Istanbul, November 1987 (p. 104).

These policies resulted in more upward mobility and in a large number of work opportunities.

At the outset of this mass labor migration, Turkey was slow to respond to the demand of the German labor market, a demand voiced officially by the German government. The Turkish government voiced political concern and ambivalence about the wisdom and long-term effects of sending Turks abroad as workers. At the time, the Turkish government was more interested in attracting foreign investment and, through industrial development, creating employment opportunities within the country. Part of the ambivalence was also due to the nature of the work that was demanded of Turkish migrants. Most of the work was in socially less desirable, tiresome and dirty jobs of the kind which German workers no longer wanted to do themselves. Soon, however, labor migration acquired a momentum of its own, and became more dependent on the overall pull and push factors of the receiver and sender countries than on governmental incentives on the part of the sender country.

The first Labor Exchange Agreement between Germany and Turkey was signed on September 1, 1961, at a time when Turkey was going through dramatic internal political strife and political adjustments. The first group of Turkish workers to arrive in Germany was greeted cheerfully and enthusiastically by the German authorities and society at large. As for the Turks, this heralded the opening of a new labor market which promised prosperity and the acquisition and accumulation of capital at a time when Turkey was entering decades of rising unemployment, rural-to-urban migration and unplanned urbanization. Soon, working in Germany became a dream and hope for thousands of Turkish villagers and rural migrants clustered in large cities. Labor migration of this type into industrial countries has been described as "a remarkable though greatly unnoticed symbiosis of interest...evident between those individuals seeking escape from poverty and those who need their hands and effort."[5]

As negotiations proceeded between the two countries, Germany became impatient and even threatened to seek laborers elsewhere if Turkey were not quick to provide a sufficient number of workers. In August 1965, the President of the German Employers' Association gave a speech to one of the leading Turkish daily papers (*Milliyet*). He said,

> We have asked for 200,000 workers from Turkey.
> However, the recruitment is progressing too slowly.
> If this situation does not improve, we will seek
> workers from countries like Spain and Portugal.[6]

Initially, demand for employment led to the export of a significant portion of the young, active male population. Later, however, as industry in Europe continued to employ out-of-date industrial equipment and offer lower wages, there was a rising demand for the employment of female migrant workers, particularly in the manufacturing, iron and metal industries. More specifically, female workers were concentrated in electronics, the automotive industry, textiles,

---

[5]Galbraith, J.K. *The Nature of Mass Poverty*, Harvard University Press, 1979 (p. 119).
[6]Birand, M.A., *Türkiye'nin Ortak Pazar Macerasi*, (The Turkish Adventure into the Common Market 1959–85), *Milliyet Yayinlari*, 1985, (p. 4).

chemical production, food processing and packaging as well as in cleaning services.

Official Turkish workers went through a laborious recruitment process which also involved a thorough medical check-up before being admitted into the quota of workers. Many applicants failed to pass this screening process. Initially, Turkish workers were not allowed to bring their families with them. Most spouses (men and women) and children waited in Turkey for the necessary lapse of time before being called to join their wives, husbands or parent(s) working in Germany. While the money sent by the workers was welcomed by the families left behind and also by the Turkish government, which more and more counted on the revenues provided by this expatriate labor force, the hardships of separation and life conditions for Turkish workers living and working in a European country began to leave an irreversible mark on all involved.

At individual levels, the numbers of marital separations and divorces increased as did extra-marital unions, especially for those living in Germany. The children of the migrant workers were the most affected group. Although these material conditions improved, the social environment in which they grew became more complex and often ridden with conflict. In many cases, children were at temporarily left in Turkey, where they lived with relatives or were placed in institutions without the direct and intimate care of their parents. Many cases of neglect or abuse have been documented.

Various difficulties awaited children taken to or born in Germany. Girls especially became the target of parental conservatism. Many migrant parents wanted to raise their children in an atmosphere which they believed to be one of authentic Turkish traditional values and culture. Children have had to reconcile the realities of studying in German schools, embedded in German society, while at the same time living in a home distinctly separate and in many ways alienated from mainstream German culture. Almost invariably, upon return to Turkey, such children found themselves to be outsiders in their home country, unable to fit into mainstream norms and expectations. Thus, it has been commented that these children carry their "otherness" with them across national boundaries as well as intergenerationally.[7]

The earlier honeymoon period of labor migration, shaken by the limitations imposed by economic growth, soon soured into a disenchanted co-existence as migrant Turkish workers began to inhabit German cities as well as work in factories and other work places. The famous words of the Swiss writer Max Frisch, frequently repeated in the early 1970s by politicians of all sides, sum up the subsequent outcome of the initial German expectations of labor migration into Germany: "We wanted a labor force, but instead we got human beings." The term *Gastarbeiter* (guest worker) given to migrant laborers also ironically expresses the dilemma of the foreign workers' reality. Labeling these workers as guests attributes a temporary quality to their presence in German society. It also implies a favorable reception on the part of the host country. Both are strikingly false implica-

---

[7]See Tufan, B., *Türkiye'ye Dönen Ikinci Kusak Göçmen Isçi Çocuklarinin Psiko-sosyal Durumlari*,(The psycho-social problems of the second generation children of returned migrants), TC Basbakanlik, Devlet Planlama Teskilati, Ankara, 1987.

tions since the vast majority of workers are permanently settled in Germany and are far from being treated as welcomed guests.

The phenomenon of labor migration and its problems have led economists and other social scientists as well as politicians to question the costs, benefits and long-term implications of this movement. Is the system by which such workers are recruited a convenient arrangement which brings labor to the host country, valuable foreign exchange and a reduction in unemployment to the exporting country, and a higher standard of living to the workers? Or is it one which benefits only host country employers at the expense of both the recruited workers and their home economies?[8] These questions still dominate the debate related to mass labor migration.

Since the beginnings of the 1960s, migration from Turkey to Germany has accelerated just as has overall labor migration to Western Europe. Migration reached a peak in the mid 1960s and after a short fall around 1967, grew again during the period of 1969-73. However, since the 1973-74 oil crisis and the following period of limited growth and economic stagnation, severe unemployment in the major industrial countries has meant a virtual halt of all formal recruitment of workers in all major labor importing countries.[9]

The OECD's continuous reporting system (SOPEMI) has estimated that approximately 80,000 people returned to Turkey from

---

[8]See Paine, S., *Exporting Workers, The Turkish Case*, University of Cambridge, Department of Applied Economics, Occasional Paper 41, Cambridge University Press, 1974, and Philip L. Martin, *The Unfinished Story: Turkish Labour Migration to Western Europe, With Special Reference to the Federal Republic of Germany*, 1991.

[9] Kazgan, G., *Prospects for Turkey's Accession to the Community*, (Report for SIAR: Social and Economic Research Inc.), Istanbul, November 1987.

Western Europe between 1974 and 1976. However, these figures and the abrupt halt of labor migration into Western Europe should not be interpreted as the complete end of migration flow. Since 1974, the migration flow from Turkey has been characterized by three aspects: First, an increased migration of non-actives, which is the result of family reunification policies which had began earlier. Second, a decrease of return migration from Western Europe to Turkey. Third, and maybe most significant, a continuously increasing growth of the Turkish population in Germany as a result of the high birth rate among migrants and the emergence of second and third generation Turks as foreign residents in the receiver countries. The proportion of second generation Turks is high. The cohort between age 0-6 (201,500) and age 7-18 (382,900) exceeded 39 percent in the early 1980s.[10] More than half of the foreign children in Germany are Turkish children and almost 60% of all foreign students are Turks.

The presence of large numbers of Turks, described as "a highly visible and predominantly non-integrated ethnic group" in Germany in recent years has been the focus of growing feelings of animosity and even open racism. Although highly praised in the beginning for being hard-working and good-natured, Turkish workers received a negative image as time passed. Magazines and the daily press frequently report the harassment of Turks resulting from racist tendencies. *Türken raus* (Turks out) is a common graffiti on city walls. The Turkish media regularly gives news of incidences such a neo-Nazi

---

[10] Kraus, B. "Die Schulsituation der Türkischen Kinder," *Deutsch-Türkische Gesellschaft Mitteilungen*, Heft 105 (p. 3).

groups beating Turkish workers,[11] border policemen deterring Turkish citizens illegally and with hostility,[12] and random Turkish inhabitants being the target of physical violence in Germany.[13] Some Turkish communities have to employ their own youth for self-protection against hostile and aggressive groups. The daily paper *Milliyet* reports that the governor of the province of Bavaria, during his visit to Turkey, asked the help of specialists from Turkey in dealing with xenophobic and racist tendencies in Germany.[14] The *Hürriyet* headline stated that every third German would rather not have Turks in their community.

Many Turkish and foreign reporters comment that the feelings against Turks are reminiscent of those experienced by pre-war Jews. Such widespread negative treatment of Turks in Germany is an example of contemporary human rights abuses and deserves attention in its own right.[15] In terms of politics, human-rights issues related to Turkish residents also involve issues of democratic participation and full citizenship rights.[16] This becomes all the more pertinent for Turkish immigrants who are permanent residents in Germany.

In theory, the Turkish community is faced with two difficult alternatives. On the one side, xenophobic tendencies and restrictive policies in Germany lead them to contemplate a return to their home

---

[11]*Bugün*, March 16th, 1989.
[12]*Hürriyet*, February, 22nd, 1989.
[13]*Cumhuriyet*, December 7th, 1988.
[14]*Milliyet*, July 30th, 1989.
[15]See Kapani, M., *Insan Haklarinin Uluslararasi Boyutlari*, (International Aspects of Human Rights), Bilgi Yayinevi, 1987.
[16]Bendix, J., "On the rights of foreign workers in West Germany," in *Turkish Workers in Europe*, ed. I. Basgöz, Indiana University Press, 1985.

country. On the other side, harsh economic conditions and structural unemployment in Turkey force them to delay their return. Return is more difficult and problematic for second generation Turks and for all as time passes. In practice, the majority do not intend to return. An opinion poll indicates that more than half of the Turkish workers and almost all the second generation born in Germany would prefer to stay and live in Germany rather than return to Turkey.[17]

In view of the above reality, we are faced with a remarkable myth. On the one hand, from the German point of view the workers are seen to be indispensable. The time when they will not be needed is hard to envisage. Yet, there is an elaborately cultivated illusion that the migrants are only temporarily present, will never become full members of the community, and must one day go home. Their temporary status is celebrated, by their name as "guest workers." Guests of course, never outstay their welcome.

However, were these workers to depart, the German economy would be in grave peril. The great Siemens plants in Berlin, among the largest in Europe, would close down. Automobile production would come to a near halt. In 1976, some four-fifths of the assembly-line workers at the huge Cologne works of Ford were Turks.[18] Galbraith notes that when in autumn 1976 he asked a director of German Ford in Düsseldorf if the company could survive without the Turks, the director was appalled by the thought.

This situation, of course, is not unique to Germany. In other parts of Europe and the United States also, not only factory work but

---

[17]Dr. Demirbas, quoted in *Hürriyet*, March 3, 1989.
[18]Galbraith, p. 129-32.

construction work, the care provided to the sick in hospitals, and the services given in hotels would all suffer drastically in the absence of immigrant workers. If all the illegals in the United States suddenly returned home, the effect on the American economy would be quite disastrous. A large amount of useful, if often tedious, work in New York and other northern cities would go unperformed. Fruits and vegetables in Florida, Texas, and California would go unharvested. Food prices would rise spectacularly. Without Mexicans, the American economy would suffer, the way the German economy would suffer without Turks, Yugoslavs and Italians.

Labor migration has helped the economies of the host countries in more ways than simply increasing productivity. Given the positive contributions of immigrant workers, one is driven to ask why so many in host countries react negatively to their presence. One widespread feeling is that they take jobs away from native-born workers. However, contrary to popular accusations, foreign workers have helped maintain both stable prices and the relatively full employment of native-born workers because the employment of the latter can be pressed to the limit while the foreign workers are used to fill out the areas of shortage that would otherwise result in inflationary bidding for labor. Furthermore, native-born workers, and indeed second generation immigrants, do not want to do the type of jobs that new immigrants are willing to do. Thus, we cannot easily talk of immigrants taking away wanted jobs. German, Swiss and Austrian unions agree that migrant workers are not hampering the employment chances of native workers.

The use of foreign labor has also kept unemployment figures distorted in the host countries. The unneeded and unemployed workers of Britain or the United States reside in the countries and can be counted, but the surplus of Germany and Switzerland are in Turkey, southern Italy, or Yugoslavia, safely beyond the statistics.

As for the native countries, migration is seen to be one of the remedies against the vicious circle of poverty. Nevertheless, the sender countries lose those members of society who are most motivated to escape the grip of poverty. Millions of immigrants (from Poland, Germany, Italy, non-Jews in the Russian Empire, the Balkan States) rejected accommodation and made their escape, mainly to the United States. All who so moved, almost without exception, bettered their position.[19]

This exodus from the old world is recorded in history and carries an aura of heroism with it. However, what is not acknowledged is that the process still continues today on an even greater scale: In Europe they are called immigrant workers, in the United States they are the illegal immigrants. Nevertheless, there is a difference between the earlier and the present migration movements:

> ...Once when those rejecting accommodation arrived in the new country, they were there for good. They came with their families; there was no thought of return; they merged with the established population or the earlier arrivals, became citizens, voters, and eventually full participants in the society.
> ...(Today) they share the ancient characteristics of having found an effective escape from the equilibrium of poverty into which they were born, of con-

---

[19]Galbraith, p. 123.

tributing greatly to the well-being of the countries to which they go, and of being regarded, withal, with the greatest unease.[20]

Migration of the above-described scale and nature from Turkey to Germany has created a subculture that carries its own idiosyncratic features. *Please, No Police*, the novel which follows, is one artistic expression of that subculture. But the migrant experience has given rise to many diverse forms of art. Turkish cartoons showed the first workers, popularly known as *Alamancilar* ((literally and colloquially meaning "those of Germany"), as men wearing a feathered green or beige hat known as the "Hans hat" and carrying in their hands a loud transistor radio as they walk the streets. The lives of these workers and their families who migrated to Germany, or of those who were left behind in Turkey slowly became a new subject matter for films, plays, novels [21] and poetry as well as journalistic accounts and social science research. This was true not only in the Turkish language but also in German.

The past three decades have been rich in the production of commercial films related to this labor exodus. Some German producers such as in the films *Yasemin* and *Sirin's Wedding* chose to dwell on issues revolving around Turkish migrants' unwillingness to give up traditional values. But other works by Turkish producers like Tevfik Baser's *Germany in Forty Square Meters* and *Goodbye to a False Heaven* have adopted a feminine perspective, examining prob-

---

[20]Galbraith, p. 126.
[21]See for example, Dayioglu, G., *Geride Kalanlar* (Those Left Behind), Bilgi Basimevi, Ankara, 1975 and by the same author, *Geriye Dönenler* (The Returned Ones), Altin Kitaplar Yayinevi, Istanbul, 1986.

xxi

lems of adaptation and alienation experienced by Turkish migrant women coming from and entering into a different but nevertheless strongly patriarchal culture. Other notable films which have migrant workers as their subject matter include Fassbinder's *Fear Conquers the Heart*, Schroeter's *Palemo Wolfsbourg* and Sholimowski's *Success at all Cost*. Serif Gönen's *Germany, the Painful Homeland* and *Polizei* try to make a political critique by giving sketches of Turkish migrants' daily lives.[22]

Turkish labor migration has also led to much journalistic narrative documentation. Predominant among this genre is Günter Walraff's work, *Those at the Bottom*, where Walraff relates his experiences when he sought employment disguised as a Turk. His personal experiences first appeared as a provocative book critical of German prejudice against foreigners in general and Turks in particular. Subsequently, the book was made into a film.[23]

Among other journalistic research and documentation are Namik Koçak and Erdinç Ispartali's series of writings entitled *Gönüllü Türk Köleleri* (Voluntary Turkish Slaves)[24] where the conditions and experiences of migrant workers are described, enumerated and illustrated with photographs and interviews. The presence of

---

[22] (The "alamancilar" in our art in the 30th year of the migration), "Göç'ün 30. yilinda sanatimizda 'Alamancilar,'" in *Milliyet Sanat Dergisi*, December 1, 1991.

[23] This actively participant form of journalism which involved role playing was later copied by the Israeli journalist Binur Yoram who disguised himself as a Palestinian and wrote a book called *My Enemy, My Self* (Penguin Books, 1989) where he related the prejudices and humiliations he encountered when he tried to first find employment and then work as a Palestinian in a Jewish Israeli society.

[24]*Hürriyet*, November, 1988.

large numbers of recent Turkish migrants into Europe has also led to a heightened sensitivity in Turkey on the image and perception of Turks abroad. Most research on this subject shows that Turks are popularly portrayed negatively as being violent, cruel and lustful, and that the treatment of women becomes a particular point of critical focus.[25]

These novels and short stories have as stated above for many years now been recognized as constituting a "sub-literature" in Turkey. But the genre's conceptualization as *Gastarbeiterliteratur* (guest worker literature) in Germany, however, has been more recent: Although foreign workers have been subjects, if not also the authors, of works in their national languages since the 1960s, the so-called *Gastarbeiterliteratur* has been largely a phenomenon of the 1980s. The concept itself is problematic beyond the euphemism of the "guest" label. Unlike what the term may initially suggest, it is predominantly written neither by nor for the "guest workers." The literature is written mostly by intellectuals and has a reading market which includes few workers.

Critics have suggested that this literature gives Germans the chance to experience themselves as foreigners and Germany as a foreign country. It is clear that with the emergence of a German *Gastarbeiterliteratur*, the problems, hopes, fears, anger and frustration of two generations of immigrant workers have been made more directly accessible to the German-reading public. However, the German literature of foreign workers in Germany is more than an in-

---

[25]Hadi Uluengin's series "The Image of the Turk in European Cartoons," *Avrupa Çizgi Romaninda Türk Imaji* in *Cumhuriyet*, 20 February, 1989.

stance of an exploited and marginalized group finally bringing its experience into the German public sphere; it is also an opportunity for Germans to undergo a kind of cultural "alienation effect" and to examine their attitudes and behavior toward others.

Gastarbeiterliteratur has opened a discussion of ethnicity, imperialism and class interests vis-a-vis literature. The term carries with it questions related to language differences. The concept has been developed of "small" or "minor" literature that is the collective and revolutionary literature of a minority writing in a major, dominant language. As such, written within and against a dominating literary and cultural tradition, minority literature is found to be structurally and politically related to the situation of the Third World vis-a-vis advanced industrial nations. Deleuze and Guattari state that minority status in a language and a culture that are not one's own ("the problem of a minor literature") is "the problem of immigrants, and especially of their children."[26]

Literary critics have commented on the previous silence of the foreign worker, especially that of Turks in works of contemporary German drama. The Turk is often portrayed as mute and this silence makes him indecipherable. In fact, from the German point of view, Turks have been an enigmatic, silent presence in West German society for the last twenty years. They have constituted a linguistic and cultural minority, economically and socially underprivileged. When the silent Turk begins to speak in the dominant language, to what

---

[26] Gilles Deleuze and Felix Guattari, "Kafka: Toward a Minor Literature," trans. Dana Polan, *Theory and History of Literature, vol. 30* (Minneapolis: University of Minnesota Press, 1986), in Teraoka A.A., "*Gastarbeiterliteratur*: The Other Speaks Back."

extent do his words represent a collective and oppositional consciousness of the kind envisioned by Deleuze and Guattari, one that exists, in the words of Kafka, "between the impossibility of not writing, the impossibility of writing in German, and the impossibility of writing otherwise"?[27]

In the so-called *Gastarbeiterliteratur*, the opaque "other" has broken its silence and begun to speak to the West. Moreover, in speaking the dominant language (German), it has begun to speak back. The predominant themes and issues addressed in this literature attest, in fact, to the intensity with which the authors feel the "otherness" of their existence in Germany. They speak of their isolation, of the prejudices directed at them, of their alienation not only in this foreign land but also of hostile conditions in their home land.

In her article *"Gastarbeiterliteratur:* The Other Speaks Back," Teraoka suggests a political context for analyzing this recent branch of literature in Germany. Teraoka points out that if a "guest worker literature" does not in fact exist as its name literally but erroneously implies, then we need to look at the various and conflicting projections of its identity. That is, who is it that offers a definition, what definition is offered, and—the fundamental question that underlies these inquiries—what political interests are at stake in the argument over this contested literary territory?[28]

Teraoka identifies three dominant groups that have defined *Gastarbeiterliteratur* differently. The Turkish author Pazarkaya, who

---

27 Teraoka, Arlene Akiko, *"Gastarbeiterliteratur:* The Other Speaks Back," in *The Nature and Context of Minority Discourse*, ed. Abdul R. Jan Mohamed and David Lloyd, Oxford University Press, 1990, p. 297–8.
28 Ibid.

claims to be a pioneer in this field, represents the position of cultural exchange and mutual understanding with the ultimate aim of social, as well as cultural, "synthesis." He argues for mutual recognition since migrants who earn a wealth of experience by coming to Germany have also something valuable to offer and share. From a humanistic perspective, he calls for genuine synthesis which can only come about through acquaintance with both cultures, a synthesis which can only be achieved by turning Germany into a second homeland and German culture into a second culture. He speaks of the grand German tradition of the Enlightenment, of German idealism and classicism. He even argues that this high German culture and language does not properly belong to those native speakers who abuse the values of this tradition by seeing in it a tool of humiliation and exploitation.

Thus, true German culture and true possession of the language are elevated to a sphere of moral and humanistic understanding to which anyone can aspire, regardless of nationality or native language. In this way, Pazarkaya upholds universal human values rather than cultural, national or even class differences. His position is described as unifying rather than oppositional.

A radically different position seems to be taken by the authors of the Sudwind Gastarbeiterdeutsch series. In place of harmony, or cultural synthesis, Franco Biondi and his co-workers call for political solidarity and seek to inspire resistance. Instead of appealing to the values of a humanistic Enlightenment, they concentrate on clarifying the everyday problems experienced by a largely foreign working class in Germany. Class differences and interests are promoted above national or cultural differences. Their position is largely critical and oppositional, multinational and committed to the side of the workers. German language is used only in so far as it is a pragmatic tool for multinational communication. Aesthetic concerns are subordinate to political ones.

However, like the former proponent of *Gastarbeiterliteratur*, this second group also proposes and aspires to a conciliation whereby ultimately a rapprochement and mutual acceptance are sought between Germans and guest workers. This should not, however, be seen as aspiration for cultural absorption, they say, since both groups are acutely weary of a process that may destroy identity and turn foreigners into well-assimilated, German-integrated individuals.

A third group identified by Teraoka consists of sympathetic German academics at a research institute whose object of study is German as a second language. Ackermann and Weinrich of the Institute for German as a Foreign Language at Munich University have led the way among German scholars in focusing institutional attention on the literature written by foreign workers. They welcome the challenge to German literature from outside. Sponsoring and conducting literary contests in 1980 and 1982 (judged on both occasions by a jury of all-German scholars and critics) on the themes "As a Foreigner in Germany" and "Living in Two Languages," they seek to promote foreigners to submit works in German, or better still, to start to write in German.

As such, this group's efforts are criticized for carrying colonial or rather pseudo-colonial assumptions and interests. Whereas Biondi and the Sudwind editors base their definition of a *Gastarbeiterliteratur* on the shared experiences of foreign workers in Germany, the authors of the anthologies of the third group only require the use of German as an acquired language. Thus, one ends up grouping together the child of a Turkish guest worker who grows up in Germany with the Stanford undergraduate who spends her junior year abroad in Bonn. The second area of criticism is their insistence on literariness which the critiques see as a strategy to defuse the potential force of this literature. Thirdly, Ackermann and Weinrich are criticized for attempting to incorporate this form of literature into the German tradition. By regarding it as fundamentally "German," they impose cultural hegemony and thus disarm the literature they study.

It is evident from the above analysis of *Gastarbeiterliteratur*, provocatively defined as the "other" speaking back, that this is an intricately complex area of literature perceived differently according to one's political perspective:

> (T)he category of the "Other" is laden with political, social , historical and cultural features. Its "speaking" also is never straightforward, direct, and unequivocal, but always mediated and controlled by translators, editors and academics. There is in fact no silent Other as such who now begins to speak. Rather, we must speak in terms of groups with conflicting interest who, each in their own way, seek to produce and promote a *Gastarbeiterliteratur* of their own definition. The literary phenomenon of the 1980s—the sudden outpouring of German literature written by foreigners—is first and foremost a politi-

cal battleground for recognition and for control; *Gastarbeiterliteratur* is contested territory.[29]

Aras Ören and *Please, No Police*

Aras Ören, born in Turkey in 1939, has been writing in this dynamic multicultural literary setting. He describes his arrival in Germany in his poem, "Biography:"

> I came to this town of my own free will
> In September the 9th, 1969, and settled here.
> The private reasons for my personal exile
> I will keep to myself. I guess
> What I have told you is enough.[30]

His works, highly regarded in Turkey as well as in Germany, are in the form of both prose and poetry. He has won several prizes: The Culture Prize from the Union of German Industrialists (1980), the Bavarian Academy of Fine Arts Prize (1983), and the first of the Adalbert von Chamisso Prize for resident writers in Germany (1985). *Please, No Police*, first written in Turkish and translated here from the Turkish, was originally published in German as *Bitte Nix Polizei* (1980).[31]

---

[29] Teraoka, A.A., p. 316.

[30] (Poem translated from Turkish by Gürsoy-Tezcan) in G. Emre's "30 yillik 'Alamanciligin' edebiyata yansimasi," (The reflection into literature of 30 years of being "Alamanci") in *Milliyet Sanat Dergisi*, December 1991.

[31] Since 1987, Ören's three separate pieces of work have been published in Turkish. These are (in Turkish) *Affection Lost: stories and fragments of a novel* (1987), and two novellas: *The Secret Life of "A"* (1990) and *Hollywood Nostalgia* (1991).

The novella gives us images of Berlin at different hours of the day and night. Ören is one of those rare authors who successfully combine national and international with personal politics. These he shows us as embedded in the daily details of his characters. The novella is a compelling description of social conditions shared by working class Turks and Germans. We are gradually introduced to the characters and to their settings of different work places, homes, taverns and various streets of Berlin. The plot of *Please, No Police* unfolds unobtrusively into a powerful drama. Ören's writing is at the same time humanitarian, deeply class and gender conscious, articulate about cultural and national differences, and politically provocative without giving way to simplistic sloganistic expressions.

The novella is a critical presentation of multicultural working class life in Germany, with its sad and all too familiar problems of alienation, unemployment, alcoholism and ethnic prejudice. The characters act out popular themes: The hero, Ali Itir is illegally seeking work in a cold German city. The Germans in the novel come across as materialistic, alienated (unwilling to help those who fall down), sexually permissive, hypocritical and smug. However, they are also victims: of abusive fathers, exploitative bosses and husbands, alcohol and anger. The hero, a recently arrived Turkish migrant worker is more spontaneous and readier to help those in need than are the native Germans. However, no one culture or its institutions are glorified. The novella is also a reflection on the conditions of life in Turkey, as the hero considers the military training he underwent in Turkey, his sexual frustrations and the petty power games of the streets of Istanbul.

XXX

The extended Turkish family (often defensively glorified as an asset for Turkish culture) is not presented in rosy colors. On the contrary, its depressing limitations are openly portrayed. We are initiated into the resentments and the humiliating insinuations directed at the hero during his stay with his cousin and his wife in Berlin. Hatçe, another character in the novel, the mother of four, induces an abortion and becomes critically ill at her work place. Ören makes us reflect on gender relations in the families in the migrant Turkish community as we learn that Hatçe knows that her husband lives also with a German woman.

An overall sensitivity and awareness of gender-related issues in the last decades has led to a new critical evaluation of cross-cultural gender interaction. What are the dynamics of male/female sexual relationships among men and women of a dominant culture and those of a minority or less dominant culture? The question becomes more complex when we also introduce social class and age differentials. Recent studies on Latin America or Asia have analyzed the imperialistic or colonial and social class dimensions of cross-cultural sexual relationships including official marriages. Although there is ample room for comment and the literature is rich with cases of cross-cultural marriages and sexual relationships among Muslim Turks and Christian Germans,[32] there is no research which focuses on this issue in an analytical way.

---

[32] Among the many examples in literature we can cite Habib Bektas' *Hamriyanim* (1989) where Fatma, the daily cleaner, falls in love with the sociologist Fritz; the *Mardin-Münih Hatti* (The Mardin-Munich Line), which is the story of the divorce between a Turk married to a German woman, a case which later became a television film in the form of a series.

Turkish (male) authors have written a number of novels on the theme of the dramatic change encountered in numerous Turkish women who go to Germany. Ümit Kaftanciouglu's *Gülamber Almanyada* (Gülamber in Germany) (1975) is the story of a young village girl who in a very short time on her return for a holiday is seen to wear mini skirts, to talk freely with men and to smoke. Nevzat Üstün's novel, *Bir Kadin* (One Woman) (1975) again dwells on the changes women undergo: Nazife, who comes to Germany on her own and spends time before her husband joins her, begins to reflect on traditional male-female relationships and to assume a different identity. *Haçça Büyüdü, Hatis Oldu* (Haçça Grew Up and Became Hatis) (1978) again dwells on the transformation of women, here mostly perceived as degenerate and negative.

In *Please, No Police*, Ören does not specifically focus on gender relations but brings a dimension of ethnicity and economic power considerations to cross-cultural sexual interaction. In the novella we have two violent sexual encounters. Interestingly, three of the characters involved in these encounters are German, and only one is Turkish. The rape of the German worker woman by her immediate boss receives no publicity or open protest.

> I heard close to my ears the crew boss Ernst Kutte's drooling whispers. I wanted to scream, but I couldn't make a sound. Besides, why should I resist? To resist was a concept that had so lost its meaning...Then, too, I needed a ration card and work. Together we fell over on something soft. (p. 84)

In contrast, the German girl, Brigitte, who enters Ali's room having agreed to make love for 20 marks, later changes her mind.

> Brigitte, not quite understanding what was going on, found herself in inexorable panic. She wanted to scream, to break loose and be free. The panting face pressing against her covered her mouth and nostrils, and she could not breathe properly...
> As Ali tried to stroke her face, Brigitte had begun to cry "Help! Police!" at the top of her voice. (116–117)

If previous literature is characterized by the "silence of the Turk," the situation is reversed in *Please, No Police*. The characters speak and we know their thoughts, their hopes, desires, their fears and dreams. We have access to their sexual fantasies, their cunning little plots and their resentments. It is almost as if the author is trying to correct earlier general misunderstandings on either side, especially the misjudgement of the acts and motives of the Turks:

> Rending the silence, a milk truck was heading toward him. "Now look here, this truck driver, the bastard's about to run over me! Hey, go on your way! Not road enough out there for you?"
> He hadn't noticed that he had wandered to the middle of the road in trying to avoid deeper snow. The truck driver, pointing his index finger to his head, said, "Got birds twittering in your head so early in the morning, eh?" (p. 36)

In fact, in the novella, it is not the reader who is left bewildered by the inner world and motives of the Turks. On the contrary, it is maybe a fellow Turk, probably a political activist student who wants to raise consciousness among illegal workers and finds instead a mute, incomprehensible audience. We have no insight into the hero's or the other listeners' thoughts when the student reads out passages from a paper to the effect that the Turkish governments' concern for workers abroad is inadequate. More than communication between Turks and Germans, the novelist looks at communication between Turkish workers and the Turkish authorities or between the lonely illegal worker and the activist who intends to raise consciousness and protect the worker, communication that seems to be cut off or enigmatic:

> "I mean, don't think that I'm defending those who brought you here, promised you work and bamboozled you..." (*These guys are so silent, that's what confuses, disconcerts him. Couldn't they react a bit!*)[33]
> "Friends, those who are sold in this way are called 'tourists' or 'illegal workers'; you are these contraband goods." (p. 30–31)

German culture is shown through the eyes of a worker still in culture shock. Such a perception highlights the ordinary but evaluates it differently. For example, the traditional Muslim sensitivity to dogs, combined with the fear induced by the German police dogs, becomes an existential problem for the hero:

> What really mattered to him was not the statements of so-and-so in the papers, but the German police using dogs to hunt down "tourists." He hadn't had any peace or tranquillity since he had heard it. These days, if he happens to see a dog, he immediately

---

[33] My italics.

changes his direction. ...(T)here the police had special dogs who could sniff out illegal workers, and
they were about to do the same here in Berlin. (p. 32)

The novella sharply portrays a general and profound lack of
communication among members in the community. The illegal
Turkish worker's inability to speak German and unfamiliarity with
German ways of life are an obvious hindrance to communication.
However, that is maybe a minor obstacle compared to that caused by
Brigitte's father's alcoholism or her boy friend Achim's inability to
hear anything she has to say due to his egotism and inherent anger.
Similarly is Frau Gramke's narrow, self-centered world and her fail-
ure to reach out to anyone even when she is in a position to help. The
silence introduced by the author is not due to the incomprehensibil-
ity of Turkish culture or the enigmatic, riddle-laden quality of the
alien Turk, but rather it is due to the juxtaposition of two different
world views, with different responses to human needs:

Chief detective Michael Heymann already felt,
through trained intuition, that no matter how much
they drove around and repeated the message, the
police would not uncover any leads. And about two
weeks ago, when they discovered three Turkish
citizens, two women and a man, murdered on the
fourth floor of an apartment,...he'd realized for the
first time in his career that he had bumped against
the deaf walls of a mode of thinking, feeling, and
living to which he was a stranger. (p. 129)

The tragic hero of the novella represents in a very articulate way
the heavy human cost of the attempt to escape poverty and reach out
for a better life. Ali Itir effectively illustrates the unfortunate ones

whose dreams are thwarted, whose hopes are extinguished by harsh and hostile social and political realities. His disappearance, (suicide? accident? murder?) is woven into a picture filled with the weight of poverty, ethnic prejudice and official or governmental indifference.

Here we have a literature of the afflicted. However, there is another side to the situation. Thousands of Turkish immigrants have not just "survived" but have somehow managed, to better their living conditions.[34] Second generation Turks are already establishing publishing houses, writing books (mostly in German), participating in public debates, and trying to reach out and meet people like them in other parts of the world. They are also developing their own businesses and employing workers themselves. They are becoming less and less interested in sending money back or investing in Turkey. As Emre rightly asks, "Which is *gurbet*: the distant, alien land? Here or there?"[35] Interestingly, this generation of Turks is labeled as *kayip kusak* (the lost generation) in Turkey. For those thousands of Turks who were born in and who are living and working in Germany the issue is now one of identity. This search for identity involves a reconciliation with their roots in homeland Turkey as well as a secure and dignified presence in contemporary Europe where national borders are losing their former political and economic meaning.

---

[34] On a more marginal level, see the brief autobiography of Gülen Yegenoglu, *Almanyadaki Yirmi Yilim*, (My Twenty Years in Germany), *Milliyet Yayinlari*, 1988, where she recounts how she escaped personal and financial difficulties in Turkey by taking refuge in Germany and working there for a good part of her life.

[35] Emre, G., "30 yillik 'Alamanciligin' edebiyata yansimasi" (The reflection into literature of 30 years of being "Alamanci), in *Milliyet Sanat Dergisi*, December 1991.

The intense social tensions and conflicts presently experienced by Turks and other ethnic groups in Germany should not be viewed and treated as a unique social phenomenon afflicting German society or Turks alone. Social disturbance and conflict have usually followed mass movement from poorer to richer countries, and such conflict is often mistakenly assumed to be a permanent affliction. Galbraith reminds us, optimistically, that few realize how quickly acculturation occurs, how soon the tension subsides. We are also reminded that the real challenge of *Gastarbeiterliteratur* in Germany is to alter the prevalent dominant structures significantly. The presence and recognition of this literature means that German culture and society are no longer just for Germans. Racial purity makes way for ethnic and cultural plurality.[36] *Please, No Police* is a beautifully written account of this difficult and painful but probably inevitable social process which hopefully will ultimately result in a more harmonious multicultural co-existence.

Akile Gürsoy Tezcan
Marmara University, Istanbul

---

[36] Teraoka, A.A., (p. 317-318)

Chapter 1

It was a flower, perhaps one not ordinarily seen, a distinctive flower. I suppose what matters is not its precise shape or species, rather that Frau Gramke was dreaming of a flower that night. Say a flower, then: crown-like white petals on a wispy stem; yes, a large bloom on a delicate stalk. And those crown-like petals, if you so much as touch them, it seems they'll fall apart into your hand; between your fingers, such a sensation of crushing! And what remains on your hand is something like dust, a damp feeling.

First a tiny thing in Gramke's dream, the flower suddenly begins to shoot up and grow larger. And the air is so redolent with the yellow pollen floating up from the anther that once it slips into the nasal cavity, it makes one feel a quaint pleasure: something akin to feeling faint, starting deep inside the nose, spreading throughout the body, engulfing it, making it tremble, shudder.

Frau Gramke too feels this pleasure. The flower in her dream, she tosses and turns restlessly. As for the flower, it keeps releasing the yellow pollen from its center; the specks swarm in the air…

When she woke up her mouth felt slightly acrid, her hair was damp with sweat. Her hands were between her legs, her legs drawn toward her stomach. She unwittingly nudged the blanket covering her head, and she instantly felt the cold settle on her neck, above her nightgown. She pulled the blanket up again, this time to her nose. She remained for a while in that faltering state between sleep and wakefulness. If she allowed herself, she'd easily fall asleep again.

1

Next to her, Bruno Gramke still slept his restive sleep, unaware that she was awake. Eyes closed, he rolled his tongue, smacked his lips, swallowed several times, then exhaled deeply and buried his head a bit further into his pillow. A heavy odor of beer brushed Frau Gramke's face. This breath smelling of beer, of soured alcohol, which greeted her face as she awakened every day she had for years now gotten used to, a reality she had been inured to—the reality of an irascible, peevish, and for how long now her jobless husband Bruno, living on welfare... She gazed at him with vacant eyes: with neither pity, nor compassion, nor love, nor hatred, neither contempt nor admiration; her gaze had none of these, nothing in it. Bruno had stuck one hand under his cheek, the wrinkles in the pillow had deepened the lines on his face.

For his part, if Bruno Gramke could choose a dream now, surely he'd choose this: The moon is out. The narrow dirt road stretches from the Soviet occupied sector toward the west. The moon lights the bare branches of the beeches lining both sides of the road. A rucksack on his back, a hardy and vigorous Bruno has walked for days trudging through mud, his feet like lead ingots from fatigue, he feeling now dizzy, now nauseous with hunger... If he can only reach the West in this ragged, shabby immigrant crowd, if he can only reach the West, these nightmare days too will end. He'll make a new, a brand new start! With a full stomach, plenty of American cigarettes, and above all, brimming with hope.

Yes, if he could choose a dream now, he'd choose this. Because the road in this dream was a highway leading from point zero to innumerable promises and yearnings. Never ending. But this other

2

dream would do as well: The year is 1952. For some time now he's been seeing Greta Herbolzheimer. She too is absolutely bent on making a successful new start in life. She takes any job she can find. Then comes the birth of their first daughter, buying their first radio, iron and pressure cooker—all secondhand, but that's all right. And then about as much meat, vegetables, and butter as you can eat. Immigrants from the Soviet occupied sector are to be given priority in government housing. But why should Bruno wait? I've got a good trade, and even if I'm not at it now, he thinks, it promises much for tomorrow.

Great passions for times to come are being celebrated. It is the opening day of Kreuzberg festival days, probably August: flower and crepe-paper bedecked vehicles parade down Wrangel Street, heading for Viktoria Park, among the applause of spectators. There are bands playing, hands clapping, huzzahs of joy; the whole town, everyone, is out on the streets. Even if not all the ruins around the park have yet been razed, the desire to forget has, like a sponge, wiped off the bitter days; the war and its aftermath forgotten for now, there's dancing, beer drinking, sausages are munched, the moon is out again, and the horse chestnut trees are crowned with light...

What they celebrated was that new beginning promising so much to all. But three more years would pass before Bruno could find a more permanent job at a garment factory, enabling him to show all his skill in his trade. When he finally found it, how happy he was the morning he started, turning over those bolts of cloth one after another on the cutting table. Wouldn't he be right to choose these days for a dream now?

When Frau Gramke got out of bed, it was close to four-thirty. She gathered up her clothes, which she had flung haphazardly on the chest by the door the night before. The bedroom led to the living room. In the living room, her feet snagged on something; she stumbled, thrust her taut hands in space, as if she were looking for something to grab on to, and regained her balance with difficulty.

"You dimwit, pick up this trash of yours from under my feet," she grumbled to her daughter sleeping on the couch.

Raising her head slightly under the blanket, Brigitte muttered, "Oh, shut up, don't you see I'm still sleeping?"

Frau Gramke irritably kicked aside her daughter's handbag and shoes.

"Hey, can't you be quiet, huh?" the girl muttered again, and then turned on her side slowly, deliberately.

Frau Gramke went to the kitchen, and as she did every day after getting up, stuck a cigarette between her lips, lit it, took a deep drag, and stood there indecisively for a while.

The kitchen was colder than the other rooms. The frost had formed flower shapes on the single-pane window. Frau Gramke habitually turned on the gas on three burners and lit all three. When she sat half crouched on the chair, her forehead furrowed with wrinkles. The ash on her cigarette elongated and fell on her lap, she swept it off with her hand; the smoke made her squint her left eye hard. Then, she took the cigarette half stuck on her lips and put it out under the faucet. Mechanically, she took out of the cabi-

4

net the pink flowered porcelain coffee cups, filled the kettle, put it on the stove, and prepared the filter.

Halfway through this, as if she suddenly remembered something, she hurried to the hat stand, put her overcoat over her shoulders, picked up the keys from the nail behind the door. When she was just about to step out, she heard footsteps on the stairs, and she changed her mind about going down to the shared bathroom by the landing. "That old codger in the apartment across the hall probably just went down to empty his chamber pot, and the place stinks to high heaven," she thought.

The nine-by-twelve kitchen was now pleasantly warm; the flower shapes of frost on the single-pane window overlooking the courtyard in the back were thawing at the edges.

Frau Gramke hurried to the sink, gathered her skirt and raised herself as high as she could on her toes, crossed her left leg over the sink and halfway perched over it to piss. When she finished, she turned on the faucet and ran it a bit. The coffee water was boiling. She poured it over the grounds, poured a cup for herself, and took a slurping sip. And so, in these early morning hours, every move Frau Gramke made occurred by itself, almost as if it had been programmed before, neither leaving a trace in her mind, nor carrying a trace from her mind.

The steam, slowly swirling and spiralling from the pink flowered porcelain cup, filled the whole place with the odor of fresh coffee.

From between the stove and the wall, Frau Gramke picked up the old water pail, its white glaze chipped here and there all

5

over, walked into the living room, and emptied the ashes from the tile glazed stove. She scooped up the embers and the unburnt coal briquets and shoveled them back in.

When she went out in the courtyard she felt the hair in her nostrils bristle; it was so cold again that maybe it was a dozen or so degrees below freezing today. She drew her wool coat closer to her body and checked out the trash cans; most were filled to the brim. She poured out the ashes carefully, doling them out to three cans, closed the tops quickly on the rising dust, and went down to the basement. The basement was moldy smelling, humid, with a low ceiling and vaulted brickwork walls. Where the vaults met, the iron girders showed through the plaster.

Whenever she comes down here she vaguely hears sounds resembling screams mingled with laughter, and she still cannot not forget the air-raid nights with their interminable bomb bursts. There now, she feels again the heat rising about her neck and her cheeks flushing.

She switched on the light. The basement was still only a basement, nothing different about it: cobwebbed and quiet. She filled the pail with coal briquets, picked up the wooden snow shovel as she walked out, left the pail in some obscure corner in the yard, unlocked the main door to the building and walked into the street...

Frau Greta Gramke is fifty-two years old, lives on Pückler Street in Berlin. In this building, number 12, she and her husband have been living for nine years as supervisors, so their second-floor apartment is rent-free. On this 18th day of December in 1973, it is cold, about five a.m., still pitch dark, and in the faint light around the gas street lamps the snow swirls like white moths. Now and then a burst of wind blows the light snow from one end of the street to the other.

Across the street, Markthalle, the old covered market, resembles an abandoned train station, its ironwork gate closed, its red brick walls spotted with snow blown about by the wind. As for the street, it's an ordinary street, the buildings dating to the end of the last century, with their uniquely forlorn and melancholy look, many with balconies still showing the ravage of bombs and fire. The plaster of paris ornaments on the window niches, the reliefs in their roof friezes have broken off long ago, and where the stucco has fallen off, red bricks are exposed.

The street is paved stone; the sidewalks are made of larger blocks of cut stone, all of which is now blanketed by snow. The snow on the top is granular like farina, but underneath, it is frozen solid.

Frau Gramke has been shoveling snow for almost half an hour. Her hands have turned blue, gradually losing feeling, and she talks to herself: "It's a tough winter, and this shit is more like concrete than snow, needs a pick. Who's that coming this way? Is that him again? Hmmph, he can hardly walk and he has to have a dog to drag behind him..." She shakes her head, a mocking smile on her face...

The one approaching on the sidewalk across the street with his dog like a plump cooked sausage was her neighbor from number 16. When he saw Frau Gramke, he first crossed to the sidewalk on her side, and when he was just passing her, he stopped for a moment as if this were a chance meeting. He panted and steam rose from his mouth and nostrils.

"Good morning," he said.

From his tone it was plain he wished to get a foot in the door for some sort of chat, needful or not. The dog, taking advantage of this pause, raised his leg against the puny sapling on the edge of the sidewalk and pissed several short bursts. The piss dotted the snow with yellowish little holes.

"Good morning," answered Frau Gramke, reluctantly, like someone shutting all doors to a conversation smack against another's face. Then she turned her back, showily flung several shovelfuls of snow, and said, "*Scheisse*," giving each syllable its due.

"So it is," was all the man could say; he couldn't come up with more. He mumbled a phrase or two to himself, or, more accurately, tried by mumbling to think of something to serve as an opening to a conversation. Frau Gramke had finished her shoveling and was already about to leave.

The old man turned to his dog, "C'mon, let's go, we're going," he said.

The dog, which had been sniffing around where the walls met the sidewalk, raised his head and stared at his master. The whites of its eyes had expanded, and it had a dopier look than before. "Let's go," said the old man again and tugged at the animal.

When she was just about inside, Frau Gramke turned around halfway, and like someone eager to get something necessary over with, implying she didn't like being bothered further, said goodbye to the old man.

8

Once inside, she walked out again with an irresistible urge to do so, feeling she had to look at the man walking away, not quite knowing why she did. The old man had taken some fifty or sixty steps. The dog insisted on sniffing the walls, and the man, who now wanted to cross the street, jerked its collar in the opposite direction.

Seen like this, in the distance, he looked even smaller. With his ill-fitting, obviously hand-me-down overcoat almost sweeping the ground and his Prince Heinrich cap, under the faint light of the street lamps, he was a figure between being and not being, a shadow, taking each step as though invisible strings pulled his legs, resembling something jerryrigged from a few pieces of wood—no more meaningful than that.

He was determined to cross the street. He jerked the leash harder now, and the dog bucked, but not for long, and then, giving in to his master's wish, suddenly ran toward him. The old man hadn't anticipated this; he slipped and collapsed on the curb, in the snow.

The snow kept swirling. From the other end of the street a burst of wind drove the light snow on the ground for a while. A puny sound the cold could not smother filled Frau Gramke's ears, a sound like moaning, a sound begging for help—in fact, in the stillness of the morning, a sound very discordant with the cold, the snow covered street, and somewhat comic.

The old man was struggling to stand up but couldn't manage it any way he tried. The dog was bent over his master, affectionately sniffing him about.

For a moment, Frau Gramke was apprehensive, but then with an odd spitefulness, she thought, "Let him sit where he fell, let him choke, freeze his ass, the swine," and not pausing further, she went in, impatiently closing the heavy wooden door behind her.

Upstairs, back in the kitchen, she ate a mouthful or two, standing, and dressed hurriedly. Then she spread some butter and liverwurst on a slice of bread. On another she placed two slices of salami, cut them in the middle and doubled them, wrapped them in butcher paper and placed them in her bag along with a banana. She lit a cigarette and after a drag or two put it out. In the living room now, she began to prod Brigitte, who was still sleeping.

"Get up, you sluggard. It's almost six."

Brigitte grumbled reluctantly; she had no intention of getting up.

"Let me be, will you!"

"C'mon, get up. Enough already..."

"I said let me be!"

"It's almost six."

"I get it, I get it... I'm getting up."

This last response calmed Frau Gramke. In her peculiar way of being affectionate, she said: "I left two marks on the table in the kitchen, but this is the last time... And put it in your bag before your father sees it."

"Thanks."

"And don't be late. Don't you go back to sleep when I leave now, either."

"Oooh, cut it out, will you? I said I won't, here... I'm getting up."

Frau Gramke was heard to murmur unintelligibly, open the door, and then quietly close it.

Chapter 2

However you look at it, an irremediable situation: she's awake now, but how she wishes she could sleep. No, not that she's ever had any difficulty falling asleep. On the contrary, once she gets in bed and turns her back, lying on her side, that's it. In the mornings, whenever her mother wakes her up, if it were up to her, she'd close her eyes and easily go right back to sleep.

Every morning the same thing: Brigitte cannot decide whether to get up or not. And lately, her will to disobey always weighs heavier. A persistence, a compulsion within, to do what she wishes despite everything—like not getting up now—grows ever more powerful. But then each time, whether she's indecisive or what, she gives in, she gets up and gets dressed reluctantly. She drinks a cup of the coffee her mother made, now only warm, eats a slice of bread spread with raspberry jam, then prepares her father's breakfast.

She doesn't have breakfast with her father much. If they sit down to breakfast together, they'll find an excuse to quarrel; so, it's best to stay out of one another's way. As soon as she can, she rushes out of the apartment. She does this every morning, and once she's out, she's no longer irresolute. There's no more fear, or stress from that fear, of her parents. If she likes, she might not go to work at the hairdresser where she is apprenticed. Though she has never not gone, well, she might not if she just doesn't want to.

She closed her eyes for a moment, wishing to think of nothing, to fall asleep once again. It didn't work. Her mother has surely left; she heard her close the door, and by now she must already be at the U-Bahn stop. This morning, for some reason, Brigitte keeps imagining all sorts of unlikely things. What if her mother comes back and finds her in bed? Not likely, but it might happen. maybe she's forgotten something, or remembered to tell her something—it just might happen. There's another commotion and uproar for you. Nope, she can't take that, her mother's batting eyes as she lets out an hysterical shriek, those merciless words hurled in a single breath, like an uninterrupted scream.

As if to free herself of the dialogue burgeoning in her mind, of certain situations fluttering in her mind's eye, of always trying to search for an answer in such situations, of having to listen to her mother's salvos because she cannot think of a response, of her father's unpredictable flare-ups in his drunkenness, and if he can't restrain himself, of the smack or two he gives her; as if to be free of all these, Brigitte buried her head deeper into her pillow. The more she escapes or desires to escape like this, the more a fiend appears before her eyes, in her mind, as if it were dancing, stomping around, announcing the tidings of its victory. And now the last thing she needs to be reminded of: the row last night. She sidled to it once again, this early in the morning; no, not quite—the row itself emerged from among a host of broken bits of life in this apartment with her mother, father, and sister, and stuck to her.

...And why that row last night? I came home too late, and if I keep this up I won't be able to hold down a job. I ought to be like my sister. See how she's become such a fine hairdresser, making plenty of money too. Though they know she works in a massage parlor, they act and talk as if they don't. What matters is that she makes money and gives them fifty marks a week. "Our elder daughter became a coiffurist, makes very good money. Last summer, they vacationed in the Canary Islands. That is, she and her fiancé of course!"

The man they call her fiancé is her pimp. What they really care about isn't whether I hold down a job or not but my making money; if I make money I won't be a burden to them. As for "You came home late," it's an excuse; all their worry is I won't be able to get up early enough for work and get fired. I ask them for a mark or two once in a while, that's why they do all this...

If it were up to her, she could sleep at least another hour. Her work started at eight thirty, but she had to get up before her father did, pick up her bedding, remake the coffee and prepare breakfast. Because he was unemployed, her father could sleep in a little longer. The boundary of this "little" was the inviolable one of custom; you simply did not sleep till eight during the week. It was impossible to see either her mother or father transgress the routine they were accustomed to. And not only did they themselves not transgress, they could not bear anyone else doing it. The cup they tried to force on her contained their own fear.

Brigitte got up, pressed her back against the tile-glazed stove, and let the spreading warmth permeate her body with pleasure. She put on her pantyhose, straightened her hair with her fingers. As she withdrew her back from the stove and walked to the kitchen, she put on her sixteen-year-old face, and that harsh look peculiar to her, hiding there. "I don't want to be like them, like anyone!"

14

Inside her, a new wave of rebellion rolled over the last and swelled again: she does not want her mother to wake her up mornings; she does not want to see her father when he gets up, standing there in his pajamas, his nose beet-red from drinking the night before, his belly distended; she does not want Frau Lieselotte, the owner of the beauty salon, to say "Do this this way, and that that way," and, with her dyed red hair and overdone face and eyes, to direct and inspect whatever Brigitte has to do and with what demeanor; nights, especially on cold winter nights, to have to sit before the TV set in the only heated room of the apartment; to hear her father, irritated by a TV commentary, hold forth, then get up in a huff and without asking anyone switch the channel.

Worst of all, she can't express any of these feelings. It's as if she lacks all ability to express herself, as if she can't find the necessary words. When she doesn't like something, it always comes out in answers with the same set words:

"Pass me the TV magazine."

"Here," she flings the magazine before her mother.

"What's the matter with you? Why do you act like this?"

"What's it to you?"

"You don't have to be rude!'

And on the heels of this, innuendoes loaded with threats. "Get the hell out if you don't like it!" Brigitte can only respond with something to deflect these, which increases the tension: "Shut your mouth, don't bother me!"

What really disconcerts Brigitte is that, after such bouts of recalcitrance, she herself can't figure out how things should be either. If she left now, where she'd go or how she'd live is not that important; rather, will she then be free from what she loathes, what she'd rather not have happen?

Let's say she leaves, she and Achim rent an apartment, and then what'll she do? What will the apartment be like, with what sort of furniture? What will they live on? Achim will still be going to work and so will she. Let's say Achim has completed his apprenticeship and passed his master mechanic test, and he's working as a car mechanic some place. As for herself, Brigitte can imagine herself working only as a beautician, despite all her resistance to it, all her dislike of it.

Next, she imagines getting pregnant, having children and so on, as well. Achim has sold his Honda motorcyle and bought a car. They have an apartment with its own bathroom in a new building with central heating, not one with a stove and a shared bathroom. In the living room there's a china cabinet covering one whole wall of the room; the TV set is color and the latest model; a 120-watt stereo system is in its proper place; and they even have a recessed night lamp and a built-in radio in their imitation leopard-skin covered bed.

They spend their annual vacations in Costa Brava. In the mornings, they breakfast together and leave home together. Achim drives her to work, and they kiss when they part. No, this leaving together won't happen. Because Brigitte must be at work at eight-thirty and Achim starts at seven at the latest. So, they can't leave home together in the mornings; she has to take the U-Bahn to work.

16

The linked dream breaks down here. Whenever Brigitte starts to fancy a life she'd like for herself, lo and behold, she finds herself imagining the life she loathes, only with different furnishings, in a different place and time but essentially the same as that of her parents. Then her dream snags on some totally unexpected detail, breaks off, fragments and scatters.

What led up the the row last night? It was Monday, and Mondays Brigitte doesn't work, since beauty salons are closed. She and Achim had planned to meet at their usual hangout on the Saturday before, but she couldn't leave, because her sister and her pimp had come over to visit and have coffee, and stayed longer than usual. When they left, it was almost ten p.m. Then Sunday, too, she had to stay home all day, and only Monday afternoon had she been able to go out to the cafe where Achim and her friends hung out.

The cafe was the usual cafe, nothing special about it. And in its stale frying-oil-smelling air, there was nothing other than the ordinary, nor anything unusual about the man behind the counter with his pimpled face and childlike expression.

A man in his mid-sixties was constantly feeding the pinball machine by the entrance with fifty pfennigs, ten pfennigs, intently watching the wheels turn and lights go on and off, and urgently pressing the buttons as if he were doing something very serious and important. The hoops that seemed to stop started revolving again, and the lights blinked on and off. Now and then the old man turned his back to the machine, as if it were of no consequence, and reaching over to the counter, took a few sips from his beer bottle. There

17

was a certain ease in the way the man drank, and he enjoyed the counterfeit delight of assuming that he made a machine—which worked outside its own will, and only when fed coins—do what he wanted it to do.

Brigitte recognized this man. He frequently sat with her father at Pückler corner tavern at the entrance to the Markthalle, drank beer, played dice, or stood before the tobacconist's shop, having a friendly chat with the owner. Ever since his retirement, he never tired of spending his days between the triangle of the tobacconist, the cafe, and the beer hall, wagging about what he saw and heard between the three places.

He had extravagant opinions on just about everyone. Let someone mention anything, he'd offer pompous speculations about it endlessly. Even if they paid attention to him for a while and he would a bit later bore everyone, he invariably attracted listeners; they couldn't help it. Sometimes, after they'd had enough, they'd mock him, then plainly tell him to get lost. And if he were at the beerhall, he'd pull himself together in a hangdog way and head for Schmittchen the tobacconist's. If he were at the tobacconist's, he'd go to the café, where, past the occasional rude remark they hurled at him, the youthful crowd with whom he hadn't been able to establish any ties gathered, he'd amuse himself with the pinball machine.

When Brigitte entered, she'd asked the man behind the counter busy wiping the showcase whether anyone from her crowd had been in. The man had said, "They were all here yesterday. Asked about you," and had grinned annoyingly. Brigitte had noticed for the first time that he had large, detergent-roughened hands with stumpy fingers.

...I sat at one of the two tables in the far end of the cafe and ordered a Coke. A little later Frank came. He wore tobacco brown overalls; on the chest pocket there was a patch which said "Honda" in a graceful script. He'd done this to rile Achim. Frank is a funny guy; it's as if his only striving in life is to make people laugh, to have fun with what others take seriously.

"Well now, everyone loves a Honda, everybody's got a passion for a Honda, and me, I've got it too."

"Why don't you have a seat?"

"Can I refuse when a sweet girl like you asks me sit down? No way! Where're we headed? Vroom, vroom"...

Frank sat astride the chair with its back toward him, pretending to drive a motorcycle, twisting the throttle back and forth, imitating Achim: "It's marvelous, isn't it? Now look, see how it takes off, watch this getaway!"

Bouts of exaggerated laughter from Brigitte. Even if she were pretending, she meant to prove she was playing along. Achim had caught them in this mood when he walked in suddenly. He frowned, his cheek muscles twitched nervously, and he ordered a Coke without greeting either of them. There was now an unpleasant atmosphere, silence, and only the repeated clinking of the coins dropping in the pinball machine breaking the silence. Having finished his drink with one tilt of the bottle, Achim had grabbed Brigitte by her wrist and dragged her after him. And Frank had sat there motionless. Brigitte remembers only that when she was

19

trying to settle into the backseat of the motorcycle her eyes met Frank's, he sitting at the far end of the cafe, still as an idol; then she smiled at him, which he did not notice.

...It wasn't clear what Achim was about to do. When I said "What's going on?" he said, "Wait, you'll see." I sat on the back. He drove fast, impatiently. I held on tight to his waist. The snow and the cold, rough wind kept me from opening my eyes.

At Kottbusseer Gate, under the U-Bahn overpass the cycle skidded on the wide curve heading toward Kottbusser Boulevard, and we almost took a spill. I held on tighter to his waist and in a faint cry I told him to slow down, but he ignored me. I remember feeling my palms sweat in all that cold. To protect my face from the wind and snow, I'd turned my head sideways, pressed my cheek snug against his back, and shut my eyes as hard as I could. Then we took a right near Hermann Square and stopped at a place soon after.

I remember too, on the first floor of the building we stopped in front of, a shop with its roll-down shutters closed. We went in. Actually, Achim entered first and I followed. He said nothing, and I asked no questions. We went through a dark corridor, came out into the courtyard, and Achim rang the bell to the ground floor of the building on the right. I don't remember how much time passed until the door opened, but it was a good while. As we waited, a Turkish woman went by, all swaddled, regarding us suspiciously. Her insistent gaze was disconcerting. She seemed about to say something, but said nothing.

A tall, thin man opened the door. Achim and he obviously knew each other; they shook hands. The man invited us in, and we went through a long hallway with a coconut-mat floor to a medium sized room. It had an oddness, an air about it I'm not sure I can convey—a mixture of the impersonal, uninviting atmosphere of medical examining rooms and the annoying feeling those unmatched pieces of furniture in bachelor apartments teem with. On an off-white, oilcloth-covered dining table, there were small bottles, items required for dressing wounds, and a desk lamp. An overgrown monstera in a small pot stood on a stand by the window. Pinned on the walls, drawn on parchment paper, were dragons, spread-winged eagles, mermaids, sailboats, and leaf-and-flower designs.

Achim talked and talked. At one point he pointed to me and said, "My girl," and then began talking again; whether I was there or not made no difference to him. That I had thought about it, that there was no chance I would later regret it, and that the man should not worry about this, he more or less assured him in my name. The man asked my age, Achim said sixteen. It was Achim who talked, kept answering, anyway.

"Where do you want it?" the man asked. Achim pointed to his own chest, between his nipples, "Right here," he said, "in the middle."

"Well, what do you think?" the man asked me, but I couldn't think of a thing to say. I couldn't pull myself together; I felt terribly uncertain. Before my eyes only fish fresh out of water kept fluttering.

"What sort of thing, then?"

21

This time, of course, he asked Achim. Achim took off his leather jacket, rolled up a sleeve to the elbow and showed him his pale blue cross tattoo. I was scared, my mouth was drying up. Achim helped me undress; no, not help, he took off my blouse and bra himself.

The man sat me down before him, adjusted the lamp so it would not shine in my eyes. The tiny needle on the small electric drill went in and out of my skin with soft strokes; its motor humming like a sewing machine numbed me. In my drowsiness, I felt as if I were tumbling into some hole. All the furniture seemed to float before my eyes in empty space: a chair, on the chair a Japanese dragon with wings outstretched, in the pot a wildly overgrown monstera, overgrown to impossible dimensions.

The thin, tall tattooist and Achim seemed to have exchanged faces, but the hands were the man's hands, not Achim's. Even the way he stretched the skin with his two fingers as the needle shuttled to and fro was soft and gentle. I must've tried to get up or something, when the needle, invisibly shuttling on my skin with soft strokes, suddenly hurt. "No moving now," the man scolded. "You've got to be absolutely still," and wiped the blood with a cotton puff.

A burning in my flesh. I felt like I was rolling down a slope. The more I tried to hang on, the more the rocks I grabbed kept sliding out of my grasp, the bushes I held on to came out roots and all. As for Achim, he towered above me, still, like a lately victorious commander: one foot slightly forward, his rough glances piercing me, one hand on the tasseled hilt of his sword—as if he were a bronze statue, not moving a hair...

22

While Brigitte brushed her hair before the mirror on the pantry door, her eye caught the tattooed cross between her breasts. As she moved her arm, the pale blue cross vaguely stretched and then tightened, as if capable of moving by itself. When she heard her father get up, she walked softly into the living room, picked up the hundred marks her sister had given her father Saturday last for Christmas expenses from the sugar container in the drawer of the china cabinet. She lost no time getting dressed.

Chapter 3

Monday night to Tuesday morning. Ali Itir again woke up with a jolt. On days he has work, he invariably wakes up like this, afraid he might be late.

All last week he'd gotten up early and gone to that shack of an office, hoping he'd find something. For days, there'd been no work. And it isn't as if he's not more than a little envious of Sultan and Ibrahim; if he had a regular job as they did, if he could set out to work without fear and anguish, he wouldn't care, would he, whether the work was hard, or fatiguing, or day shift or night shift? Then everything else would sort itself out just fine; he'd be no different from them. When he sees Sultan, swaying her big butt as she hustles behind Ibrahim on their to way work, he sizzles with envy, honestly. Can't he at least do better whatever it is she does? Is he any less hardy than they are? No, of course not, but well, he's been stamped illegal once; his papers aren't in order.

See what the stamp that baboon-faced policeman at the border put in his passport led to. Long before he started out, people had warned him, "Don't let the passport police stamp 'tourist' on your passport," but he hadn't paid much heed to it. In the end, wasn't it merely a stamp? Even if they did stamp it that way he'd find some way around it, surely. The power of one stamp lasted until there was another; by hook or crook he'd get that second stamp annulling the first. Besides, who can they find more willing than he to work in such a bustling country? He's ready to do any work they'll give him without so much as a peep out of him.

Not that he hadn't begged when his passport was stamped at the border: "Don't do this to me, brother, why I've come from so many miles away, come, don't use that stamp, who'll care, here, take this cigarette, good tobacco you know, nothing like what you've got around here, so they tell me. Here, take the whole pack, you'll have done some good in God's eyes. Look, you've pounded this stamp here on so many passports, come, skip mine, won't you? Just pretend I didn't pass through here, who's gonna lose what if you wink and imagine one Ali Itir hasn't passed through here?" Hadn't he implored and been humble? They had fallen flat, of course, these words on the ears of that baboon-faced official, but frankly he hadn't worried about the stamp much; he figured he would manage to find some way out. How could he have known, though, it was going to turn out like this!

Now for seven months he'd had to put up with this being a no-body; for seven months he was a nothing, not even a "person." No, now, to be fair, if it hadn't been for his cousin Ibrahim Gündogdu and his wife with the big butt, could he have found some roof to stick his head under—even that wouldn't have been settled either, would it now? Thank God at least for that.

When they work day shifts, it becomes all the more obvious. When they return from work he too is back, and when they sit for dinner, that Sultan woman with her innuendoes: "Well now, you know, so-and-so at the plant has a 'tourist' fellow countryman, and the guy is now a 'worker,' a real smart man he is, he's fixed things up for himself in no time, and shouldn't you try to do the same..."

...That's it, the woman thinks I'm a burden, and that jackass Ibrahim doesn't open his mouth to say a word on my behalf and then I feel even more like going right through the floor; I can't say anything, and I choke up, stymied. Well, I have to put up with it. Let me just become a regular worker once and I'll show all of you what it means to be a somebody in Germany. Let Ali Itir be the finest somebody, so all of you learn a lesson!...

He hadn't worked all last week, except yesterday they'd sent him to shovel snow off the courtyard of a factory. After work, back at the office to pick up his pay, he was told if it kept snowing he would have more work; he should come back the next morning. Yesterday morning, none of the hippie "tourists" who regularly hung around were there. Had the cold scared them, or what?

All his hopes rest on snow, so let it come down the blessed thing, let it come down! Let it bring a smile to Ali's face for a little while. When he's got a few marks in his pocket, he feels different around Sultan and Ibrahim.

It was dark all around. From where he lay, he drew apart the kitchen curtains a bit, looked out: no lights in the windows across the way and snow on the courtyard, at least a foot of it. He sighed deeply, relieved.

Last night when he came back, Sultan and Ibrahim were asleep. Since they usually returned about eleven-thirty and passed the time making tea and eating a bite or two for about an hour— maybe even more—before turning in, when Ali came in it must've surely been past one a.m. What time was it now? He'd fallen asleep as soon as he put his head down and had a jumbled mess of dreams all night.

And Sultan with her big butt had appeared in them too. She approached him, her breasts bouncing on her belly ridged with fat, and begun to bill and coo. She pressed her belly and her calves against him, holding his cheeks in her palms and, moaning, "Come give me a kiss, kiss me, my Ali, my stout Ali." Then her moans growing, "Come my Ali, my brave Ali, enter me all the way, all the way in," she kept saying. And he upended her on the bed habitually and nonchalantly and parted her legs. When her freshly shaven legs with their stubble like rows of short thistles touched his skin, he could no longer restrain himself; he stroked her legs for a long time, lost in the tingling delight in his palms.

Sultan kept pulling him toward her, her hips rolling on the bed: "Don't worry about Ibrahim, he won't dare say a word, that wimp, don't you worry," she kept begging. Ali straightened up confidently, and just when he was over her, ready to take her with all his commanding ego, his eyes caught sight of first the doll in a wedding dress by the bed, and then his gaze panned to Ibrahim sitting across in the overstuffed chair, chuckling under his breath, and just then the dream ended, smothered in darkness.

Ali worriedly touched his shorts and checked. No, he didn't have to bathe. It would've been just what he didn't need, in such cold, and in such rushed time to have to do a ritual bath.

Well, even it I had, I'd skip it this time, what would it matter, he thought. God doesn't sit up there, waiting on me, to write down sins; surely he sees how hardpressed I am. Surely he

27

sees it and waits for a chance to turn it into something favorable for me. He knows the truth: I was never a faulty servant of his, even in the service. Never minding the winter's cold nor the fear of being beaten, I always broke the ice on some crappy creek and ducked in, the important thing being to pour some water on yourself, rinse, right? Even in those days I didn't go around unclean. Things are a bit different now. I mean, even if it's cold and all, I'd do my duty, but I can't afford being late to work.

But why're you fretting so, Ali? It's all right, you don't need to wash, you checked your shorts, they're dry, no need to take a ritual bath. Darn it, why did I leave the alarm clock in their room? Serves you right Ali, let this be a lesson: go to Bilka and buy yourself an alarm clock. It's only a few marks in the end. If you had an alarm clock now, you wouldn't have to worry about having to bring it from their room, and you wouldn't have to put up with everyone's flak. I'll buy, I'll buy one for sure, if not today, tomorrow, ah if only it keeps snowing and there's work!

And why in the world had he gone to that place last night, tagging behind that rat-faced guy? What would've he missed out on, had he not gone? He would've slept a night in peace. He'd thought that, well, the fellow might help him with his predicament. After all, the squeaky wheel gets the grease; you have to try every angle; so, if it's only a threshold to hope you'll go.

It hadn't solved anything, his having gone. He was no less a "tourist" now, but then you know, any port in a storm. That young guy, some student or other, had talked, and Ali had listened with the rest.

In what was formerly a store, on whose facade it still said *An-und Verkauf*, its display window covered with tattered gauze curtains from end to end, near the corner of Spreewald Square and Wiener Street, seven or eight people sat on the edges of an odd bunch of chairs listening to the young man. At one point, the fellow took out, very ostentatiously, a newspaper from his pocket, and read aloud:

This paper, dated 6 December 6,1973, says: "The General Secretary of Confederation of Turkish Trade Unions, Halil Tunç, said: 'The government's concern for our workers abroad is inadequate.'" The article goes on to say, "General Secretary Tunç said, 'The present government cannot claim to have shown sufficient concern for the welfare of our workers abroad.' The General Secretary went on the say: 'The situation now emerging has its origin in the indifference of recent governments. These governments have been interested only in the foreign currency our workers bring back.'" And this note is appended to the news item: "On his trip to Brussels for the December 10-11 meeting of the NATO ministers' conference, Minister of Foreign Affairs, Bayülken, will confer with Walter Scheel, the West German Minister of Foreign Affairs, on the subject of Turkish workers in Germany."

After reading this, he dropped the newspaper on the table angrily and, waving his right index finger in the air, went on to talk as if he were accusing everyone before him: "Friends, those who were proud to announce as late as yesterday to have sent the seven hundred thousandth worker to Europe, those who made columns of statements to the papers on this, now seem to have changed their tune somewhat. Why? Because Germany wants no more workers, no more of Turkey's unemployed workforce, and so their fear, their frenzied worry adds up to this: what if those who came here are sent back? They keep reiterating how the state ought to be responsible toward the workers. Is the state trying to clear itself of its crime or shame of selling workers? We want jobs in our own country, we want to work there!"

Leaning forward on the table and grabbing it with both hands, perhaps imagining he was talking to a large crowd, he heavily stressed each word of his final sentence, intoned each differently and, apparently expecting his audience to be moved by this, waited for an enthusiastic response. When neither the slightest cheer nor even the least reaction was forthcoming, he seemed upset, but quickly pulling himself together, he tried to bring the issue to a head: "And friends, is it not contradiction that the state, on the one hand, supports individual initiative and, on the other, pursues entrepreneurs who join in on this sale?"

The young fellow had lost control of the situation; no one understood much of what he said. (But he must not panic. These people are all illegal workers; he must address their frame of mind.)

"I mean, the state considers the sale it makes, the making of this deal, legal, but if others do it, I mean individuals, it's not. What's sold is then considered contraband, and is so treated."

He again peered at each of the faces listening, and whether it was because it was dawning on him that they might have misunderstood his words or whatever, he went on to muddle the matter even more.

"I mean, don't think that I'm defending those who brought you here, promised you work and bamboozled you..." (These guys are so

30

mum—that's what confuses, disconcerts him. Couldn't they react a little bit?)

"Friends, those who are sold thus are called 'tourists' or 'illegal workers.' You are the contraband goods!"

Ali was trying to make concrete in his imagination what was being said, struggling to create an enemy who might be responsible for his situation. After that it would be easy: to cleanse his mind, he would assault the enemy. But, try as he might, he could not catch even a glimpse of this enemy. Every time he heard the word "state," there appeared before his eyes the face, with a high and mighty look, of a civil functionary whose clothes, talk, demeanor were nothing like his own, someone seemingly created solely to torment human beings. Sometimes it was the land appraiser in the deeds office, sometimes the health officer who frequently came to the subdistrict center but from whom he hadn't noticed any particular concern, or else a recording clerk of court. If he reflected a bit further, his memory caught sight of the sergeant over guard duty in the service, or the man at the State Employment Office who'd entered his name into the records when he applied for work in Germany, and then said, "You can't go, you don't fill the bill," devastating his hopes. ...Then, suddenly, all these faces were effaced, and his eyes met the gaze of the young fellow talking, leaning on the table before him.

He stared at the man's mouth opening and closing, the bits of saliva collecting in the corners, and marked again his words.

31

"Is not the transportation of workers, organized by the very hand of the state, in one sense the mentality of considering the individual a slave?"

Ali did not quite understand what was being said. He'd come here hoping he would find a way out of this being a "tourist." He'd assumed that he himself did not speak German, that he couldn't express himself well anyway, and these were, well, whatever else, educated people; besides, they spoke German. They'd just go and have a talk with the Germans and that'd be the end of the whole business. The meeting quite distressed him. Why did it have to be stretched out so long? Would that all this talk ended soon so he could take off; he had to get up early tomorrow.

What really mattered to him was not the statements of so-and-so in the papers, but the German police using dogs to hunt down "tourists."

He hadn't had any peace or tranquility since he'd heard it. These days, if he happens to see a dog, he immediately changes his direction. Who was it had told him, a fellow "tourist" wasn't it, that in some German city, well, whatever the name of the city—for heaven's sake, how could he remember its name now?— there, the police had special dogs who could sniff out illegal workers, and they were about to do the same here in Berlin? Of course, he says to himself, from these people you can expect all sorts of things. Why not? If they could build so many factories, so many machines, why of course they could train dogs this way.

He kept pushing the ends of his mustache with the tip of his tongue and chewed on them. He was quite annoyed; if only someone got up and left, he'd do the same.

And now, he also needed to pee. The toilet had to be there in the back somewhere. But it'd be unmannerly, Ali; no, it isn't done; you can't, when everyone is all ears, get up and go to the toilet. But then why should it be unmannerly? It's a natural need, c'mon, it'll be all right. Now Ali, get going...

The fellow next to him quietly bent over and whispered to his ear: "If you need to go, buddy, it's right there in the back: I gotta go too you see..."

God bless you.

But "No buddy, don't have to, thanks," was all that came out of his mouth.

When he left the place, the ground was pure white. The blizzard, which had begun in the afternoon had continued so late into the night without a break, had quite covered the roads, the eaves, and window niches. It was as if the breath of the whole neighborhood had frozen.

My, my, my, Ali said to himself, if it goes on like this, it's going to be mighty hard work tomorrow. My, my my...

The snowflakes swirling around the gaslights were like moths looking for a place to land, but because there was nothing to hang on to, fell, first slowly, as if defying gravity, then faster, in the lightbeams.

He'd left with the group and, walking on Lauzitser Street, they'd reached the Landwehr canal. Here, the sky was lit up, and the light settled on the tops of weeping willows. There was no sound other than the crunching of the brand new snow under their shoes. And, as it was so late and such a cold, snowy night, they did not meet anyone as they walked the length of the canal.

At Kottbusser Avenue Bridge, just when Ali was about to leave them, a sleepy car appeared from the right and drove on without paying any heed to the traffic lights in the corner, heading toward Kottbusser Gate. Halil suggested going to Bücür's tavern on Oranien Street. They all seemed to assent, but more accurately, no one objected. Perhaps Halil made the suggestion just to have said something, but since no one said a word to object, the suggestion became a common will. In fact the young fellow who'd spoken seconded the idea: "That'd be good. Let's go," or a couple of conventional words to that effect. Only Ali did not go to Bücür's tavern. Not that he didn't want to, but there were only a few hours now left to sleep, and he had to get up very early the next day.

When he tried to straighten up where he lay, he felt all his muscles ache. He swallowed a couple of times, then shook his head vigorously from side to side, rocking his body.

It's a good thing I slept instead, he thought. If I'd gone to the tavern at that hour, there's no way I'd be waking up now. Wonder what time it is?

He brought his left wrist close to his eves and peered at the faded phosphorescent numbers on his watch, but to no avail. He had to turn on the light. When he saw it was only 4:20, he gave a deep sigh of relief. He washed his mouth and gargled with water at the faucet, rubbed his teeth with his fingers. The water was cold as could be.

As he walked out, he chewed on a couple of salt-cured olives.

The U-Bahn, winding and twisting at the level of antenna laden roofs like a worm spotted with lights, approached Kottbusser Gate. Ali picked up his pace unawares. When he turned into Adalbert Street from the Kottbusser Gate intersection, he found the wind pressing on his face with all its might. The skimpy soles of his shoes were soaked from walking in fresh, deep snow. His ears felt frozen and throbbed with pain. It was bitter cold. If a pin pricked has face, especially his nose, he wouldn't notice. He tried, by turning his face and body halfway to the side, to lessen the wind beating on him.

My, my, my, he said to himself, will you look at this weather! Bitter as the cold during drills in the service!

Whenever he felt the cold in his bones like this, he thought of the service. Invariably, on those days when the cold was most unbearable, for whatever perverse reason, he would be assigned guard duty. The genuine article was the one between three and five a.m., in front of the officers' hall by the fountain. And why? It isn't proper to leave a soldier unoccupied during peacetime; he's to be ready for conditions of mobilization, etc., etc. What did guarding this fountain, this mosaic tile fountain with its paltry faucet, rifle at shoulder arms in the freezing dark, have to do with defending the country? For two whole years, yes, for exactly seven hundred and thirty days, while standing at guard duty, he'd asked this of himself and had not been able to find a sensible answer.

...There you are Ali: say you're now on guard duty, in the morning cold, real cold, between three and five. Say it's not the usual guard duty, but since you're in the lands of the infidel, say you're on a sort of guard duty. But know you're on guard duty over your own purse, for all those things you'll be able to buy, and to be the more as you own more. You're not watching over the basin and stone trough of some fountain but what gets in your purse: you're on guard duty over your own purse.

My, my, my, come down you dear, blessed snow, for the sake of Ali's bread—blow about with all your might!...

He turned his chest full face against the wind, raised his head sunk between his shoulders, as if challenging it, and stuck his chin out: "Come you infidel's cold, come on, is't you I should fear?"

Rending the silence, a milk truck was heading toward him.

"Now look here, this truck driver, the bastard's about to run me over! Hey, go on your way! Not road enough for you out there?"

He hadn't noticed that he'd wandered to the middle of the road, trying to avoid deeper snow. The truck driver, pointing his index finger to his head, said, "Got birds twittering in your head so early in the morning, eh?"

Ali jumped aside. The milk truck went on, growling away in first gear.

Chapter 4

As soon as Ali entered the office, the man who'd been sitting, reading the paper, laid it aside, got up, and said, "Well, come on in, you big Turk," in a phoney tone. "Where're your pals today?" Ali's so jittery now, every unexpected situation, demeanor, or question such as this bewilders him, spreads fear through him to every extremity. Something had to have gone wrong, some adverse event. Otherwise, why would this man ask him about his friends? On the one hand, his curiosity is working overtime, on the other, a host of questions enough to drive anyone crazy, and likely responses to such questions fast on the heel of one another, crowd his brain. After all, they were five yesterday. Had the police caught them? What could it be? Perhaps an accident. No, I'm thinking nonsense; yesterday we met after work, went to that meeting place, persuaded by that gabby student fellow, didn't we? And yes, when we left that place, we all planned to go to Bücür's tavern. They probably stayed there till early morning and couldn't get up... Now, wasn't I smart not to go along? But what if the police had collared them?

Let the word "police" enter his thoughts once, he instantly imagines himself arrested, and he can't help feeling numb and tingly all over. He began to step in place to relieve the burning sensation in his soaking wet feet, which he first felt when he entered the warm office. The snow melting on his head glided down his hair and temples. After searching to no avail for a handkerchief in all his pockets, he sort of brushed back his hair with his hands and could not refrain from shaking his body. If only he could also shake off his mind the word "police," which evoked that definite fear: not just a word, but a sign, a symbol.

The man was playing with the ballpoint pen in his hand.

"None of them came in today, but hadn't I said yesterday to all of you that you should come in tomorrow, and that if it snows there might be work?" he said almost reproachfully.

The wind behind Ali's jitters instantly subsided. Now if only his feet would quit burning. He continued to mark time, as in the service.

..."Maaark time!" An order is an order, they call it the service, they've condemned you in advance to bow the head, and now you'll do what's told, without any bucking, without so much as a peep out of you. The sergeant major had said we were a manly nation, and we proved our manliness at every opportunity by bowing to his display of it. He gets you up in the dark of dawn, you get up. "Companyyy... run!" You run, maybe a hundred of you. "Companyyy... rest!" Maybe a hundred sit down in the same instant. The one commanding is only one person, and you a hundred, but your individual will is zip, because he has these stripes on his sleeve, given him by the state...

As soon as he let the word "state" enter his imagination, he remembered last night's talk. Good for you Ali, he thought. You did well not to go to the tavern with them; see now, they did, and look what happened. They couldn't come to work this morning. Don't forget you're here on guard duty over your own purse.

Was the man, by talking about the others, teasing him? At this moment Ali can't quite figure this out. But then doesn't every sheep hang by its own leg? Even though he was only soothing himself with this thought, he felt relieved now. They should've been here. Just because, unlike them, he knows what it means to be on guard duty over his purse in this bitter cold, is it his fault they aren't here? What could he possibly do for them?

"Do you think they couldn't take the cold?"

No response from Ali. The man was bent over the desk, looking for something.

"What's your name?"

Without waiting for a response he flipped back and forth through the pages of Ali's passport. "Oh, I see, it's Ali. Right?"

"Ali."

"And your last name? I-t-i-r." He tried to pronounce it syllable by syllable.

Habitually, Ali repeated instantly: "Ali Itir." And quite unawares, he stood at attention.

"You'll go back to the place you worked yesterday."

"Yes, I'll go."

"After quitting you'll come here and get your money."

"I'll come here and get my money."

"Your passport stays here."

"It stays here."

"Some of these slick guys find work through us and then want to go on on their own, leaving us out, never thinking about the risk this business takes."

Ali didn't quite understand, but he nodded to say the man was right. If it weren't embarrassing, and if he knew the language somewhat, given the fervor brimming over inside him, he would hug him then and there. Don't you worry about the others, I'm here, you see, don't fret, be at peace! I'm ready for anything you say, just so long as you find me work, just so that you don't let Ali be shamed... Saying this, he'd then apologize on behalf of his friends, and most of all for himself.

The man was bent over the form he was filling out, and as if he adored his longhand, tracked, out of the corner of hie eye, the ballpoint pen gliding on the paper.

"You'll start at six again, like yesterday."

Then he looked at his watch as if he were giving important instructions: "It's now twenty after five. Remember, after quitting you'll come back here. You quit at quarter to five, right?"

He extended the form to Ali.

"Right."

Ali almost said, "Right, Commander," but managed to refrain. He took the form and went out.

Chapter 5

Achim's eyes remained fixed a while longer on the door through which Brigitte had entered and disappeared. One who belonged to him, proven by the cross tattooed between her breasts, the girl he loved, entered her home and closed the door on his face—the wooden, dried-shit-color double door. Achim stood there, his heavy arms hanging at his sides.

In truth, he was one who liked things in their place—everything in its place and according to some design. Only then, he'd say, you can achieve what you wanted to, get what you wanted. If he woke up one morning and all those things familiar to him weren't the way they had been, say they had changed overnight, it would distress him in a way he couldn't explain, make him edgy. This building with its yellow fiberglass awning on its third floor balcony, that window with flowers, lit up by the purplish fluorescent light, that tree, that tavern, all of these and a host of other things, whose details he did not perhaps remember at all in his daily life—if they were not all in their proper place, he would lose all his peace. And then those things he saw around him, things not in his life but which he wants: say, a color TV set, a place to live in a new building, living room furniture, stereo set, and so on, it these too disappeared suddenly, his life would be left nowhere. All these give him confidence, a direction to his life, just like an ideal. His relationship with Brigitte is like that too. Brigitte too gives him a sense of assurance; she's an inseparable part of his life. When he's around others like himself, without

41

having to say a word, he is peaceful inside. His assurance issues from her, from her being beside him, and everything fitting his design, working the way he wants it to.

They'd been to a popular spot at Lehniner Square. A little before eight, Brigitte had become restless; she'd wanted to go home. Achim too had wanted to leave, but his fear that Brigitte was cutting loose had forced him to persist in staying. Actually, he'd imagined the evening differently: they would've left this place and gone to his regular tavern and spent the evening there.

That the evening was not going just the way he wanted enraged him. He slammed his right fist against his left palm with all his might and said, *"Scheisse,"* peremptorily. He was about to turn and head for his motorcycle when he ran into the old man from number 16. The man stood there, looking curiously at him, with his navy blue cap and earmuffs, and rheum-crusted corners of eyes. He murmured something like "Good evening," and then walked away, tugging at his dog.

"This crazy geezer keeps appearing when I least expect it," Achim thought, "he pops up with his dog right under my nose. And that way of his, like he's about to make some small talk, it drives you nuts. If he wasn't so helpless I'd smash his face in; he's out all the time and everywhere, seemingly walking his damn dog!"

He walked to his motorcycle. It wouldn't start. He tried it several times, but there were only muffled putters and then silence. Achim let out another, louder "Scheisse." When the engine was about to get going, he'd carefully adjust the throttle, but then suddenly it would die. The snow had picked up pace. What did it matter if it didn't start? His place was close by. He could walk the cycle down Eisenbahn Street, just one street down from his place, but no, he was determined. He'd made up his mind he was going to start it, and that was that.

He pressed the starter once more and the engine sputtered and ran reluctantly. He turned up the throttle very carefully, using his utmost skill to keep the engine from stalling. In the freezing air the noise sounded muffled; still, the echo from the walls broke the silence of the night. He turned up the throttle one more time, and then, turning it down, jumped on the seat. When he put it in gear, the clumsy looking motorcycle wanted to leap ahead, shaking, but the snow bogged down the rear wheel, which spun in place with a wet whine.

Straddling the cycle, Achim was trying both to balance it and leaning forward and pushing with his feet to free the rear wheel. Lurching right and left, the cycle began to move. He kept switching up gears and turning up the throttle carefully. The muffled sound hung and stayed in the middle of the street.

He drove through Pückler Street, turned left to Wrangel Street at the corner with the funeral home, then took a left again to Manteuffel Street. He took the second left again, to Waldamer Street, and after another left turn, ended up in Pückler Street. There, he turned up the throttle quite a bit. So he circled several times the block where Brigitte lived, unaware of how many times.

People disturbed by all this insistent ruckus in the stillness of the night parted their curtains and looked out, and some opened their windows to see what was going on. Some not only opened their windows but began to curse into the night. Achim heard none of this. Besides even if he had, he would've ignored it. For a moment he felt quite cold: his legs, from the knees down in his leather pants, were like two solid iron rods; his hands, the tips of his toes, and inside his helmet, his nose, his ears and cheeks felt frozen. And the cycle started missing; it now misfired more and then stalled. Trundling it, he walked to Waldamer Street, parked it on the sidewalk and walked into the tavern in the corner.

As soon as he entered, a ponderously warm air smelling of beer and nicotine engulfed his face; he almost staggered. Despite the late hour the tavern was still crowded, buzzing away. Right over the counter, around the three-pronged lamp, dark blue smoke coiled.

When he entered, for a moment everyone noticed Achim, as if they knew he was coming and anticipated his arrival. Actually, Achim expected this. No one dared ask him a thing. They only stared at him. Most of the faces were familiar. Achim pretended to look at everyone, but he was looking at no one at all. His best friend, Alfred, broke from the crowd clustered around the bar and walked over to him. "Well, have you finally calmed down?" he said, and immediately added, "At this hour of the night, kid, have you gone nuts or what? Or did you have a few too many?"

The others, as if waiting for this question, seconded it with snickers, or added brief comments like, "What's happened Achim?" or "Have you gone nuts over love or what?"

When Achim hears the word love, he first feels an emptiness, and then mounting waves of rancor and rebellion roll through him.

44

If he could do it, he'd now go out, leap on his motorcycle, drive into the tavern at top speed, and watch with pleasure everyone scatter like a covey of partridges.

"Give me a half," he said, and walked over to the pinball machine.

His eyes reddened by smoke and fatigue, Alfred looked at Achim and was about to say something, but realized Achim would not listen to him now and changed his mind. He put his hands into his pants' pockets, stretched, and rising on his toes, kicked the air a couple of times. Then, regretful, he reluctantly sank into a chair by a table and swigged his half-drunk glass of beer.

Achim played pinball frantically till past midnight, and until the bartender said "Time to go," he drank beer after beer. Benno, who ran the tavern, had wiped and dried the copper-top counter long age, removed the beer taps and placed them in a glass of water, and turned up the chairs on the tables. Then he rolled down the wooden blinds inside, opened the door and pulled halfway down the metal rolldown shutter outside. From the open doorway behind the half-drawn shutter, wind mixed with fresh snow drifted in, and that made the heavy, stale air inside more noticeable.

"Thirteen halves come to eighteen marks and twenty pfennigs," he said. "Who's paying?"

Benno said this, drying his hands on his apron, half kicking them out, then picked up, between thumb and forefinger, the cigarette he'd left burning on the edge of the counter, took several deep drags, and put it out. He began to close out the cash register.

Achim ignored him; he was still at the pinball machine. Alfred nudged Achim, "Toss him a ten mark bill, c'mon we're leaving," he said. He was drowsy and tired. It was almost five-thirty in the morning, and there was no one else in the tavern. Benno picked up the money, saw them to the door and said goodbye, and closed the door behind them.

The snow had reached over a foot for some time now. They began to trundle the cycle. It was heavy, and they made way slowly. When they turned into Pückler Street, Achim suddenly fell down on his butt, along with the cycle, in the snow. A pain rose from his butt all the way to his septum, flashing lights before his eyes as if he'd taken a fist in the face. From the pain and the suddenness of it he looked confused. At first he made no response, then began to laugh, thrashing around, rolling in the snow, choking with laughter. It was not long before it got to Alfred as well. He too let himself go, and they forced themselves to keep on laughing, but their repugnant laughter was now bordering on phoney.

Alfred bent over Achim and extended his hand, saying, "Come, I'll help you."

Achim gave a jerk, and now both were in the snow. They began to laugh again, in bursts. The game went on for a while. It was Alfred who first pulled himself together, and he tried to get Achim up by grabbing him at the shoulders, "Get up, dammit, c'-mon, on your feet."

Achim kept going limp at the knees and letting his body go, all the while screaming, *"Lieber im Stehen sterben, als auf Knien leben"* out of all harmony and tune, then letting rip bursts of

46

laughter, one after another. As for Alfred, there was nothing he could do; with a wheezy voice he joined the cacophony. Then they stood up, and both pushing the motorcycle, began to walk again. The cycle felt heavier at every step and both were panting.

Pückler Street began to wake up. You could literally see the whole street wake up: the lights came on, here, over the bakery on the second floor, then in the corner building across the street, first the apartment on the left, right after that in the apartment next to it, and not long after in the two apartments on the first floor, as if by previous mutual agreement.

From number 26 a man with a briefcase walked out and immediately opened his umbrella against the blizzard.

"Good morning, sir, good morning."

So he wouldn't have to deal with a bad scene, the man blurted out a "Good morning" to Achim and Alfred, who with cracked voices were screaming nonstop, "Lieber im Stehen sterben als auf Knien leben."

Ahead of them on the curb, by the post of the purplish ringed street lamp, there was a shadowy, motionless heap. Beside it stood a dog round as a fat sausage. Achim thought he remembered the dog from some place. The images in his memory were tattered, torn to pieces; they refused to coalesce into full forms. When he got closer, he saw the heap was the geezer who always appeared as if from nowhere, living in number 16, one block down from Brigitte's.

Alfred too had seen the man around before, when he chatted with the woman egg vendor in the Markthalle, and sometimes at the corner tavern, drinking beer and schnapps about noontime, but

47

they'd never spoken. He remembers that sausage of a dog too, of course, sitting at the tavern door and staring lazily at passersby. The old codger, he may've slid and fallen in the snow, or maybe he's blind drunk. So what? You'll just pick him up, and that's all there's to it.

Achim had grabbed the old man by the shoulders and was shaking him.

"Hey look, if the guy's drunk at this hour, don't waste your strength. He won't get up until his ass freezes."

Lying there curled up on the ground, the old man murmured incomprehensibly. Achim grabbed his arms, and as he tugged at them, the man did not budge, but the sleeves of his overcoat ripped off. Alfred tried grabbing his collar, but he could not get him up on his feet either; the man felt like a sack of wet cement.

It was Alfred who first saw that someone was approaching. He nudged Achim, "Let's go," he said, "you're wasting your time; he doesn't want to get up. Besides, the cops are liable to turn up out of nowhere, and then are we in trouble: 'Who is this man? Do you know him? How do you know him? How did he get this way? How come?' See if you can answer. And then we end up with the whole thing on our hands."

Achim did not protest much. They picked up the cycle, one on each side, and took off in some hurry.

Chapter 6

The one approaching was Ali on his way to work. For a moment he'd considered turning into another street, but this was the best shortcut to the plant where he was to work. He stayed on Pückler street. He'd found this street yesterday. Besides, what had the man at the office said? "No being late, understand?" Hey, this is Ali, who all last week smarted from not having work; would he ever be late? Although he still has time—it's not quite six yet—you never know, he might just get the streets mixed up in the pitch dark of early morning. Who's he going to ask for directions then? An unexpected hitch? Why not? Just when you wanted to ask someone about it, there'd be no one around.

Wasn't that what'd happened yesterday morning? In the dark all these streets resembled one another. He knew more or less which way he should be headed, but then he'd taken a turn one block sooner, thinking it might be even a better shortcut. As it turned out, after wandering in circles, he'd ended up some place else, and deciding it was futile, had retracted his steps all the way to where he'd started at Pückler Street and followed the streets he knew until he found the plant. He'd been more than a little scared, worrying about being late to work. Yes, the best way was to go through streets he was familiar with, the right thing to do.

He'd seen, even at the entrance to the street, that something was going on at the other end.

...Oh my, to get mixed up in some fight or some such thing is the last thing you want. And you might say to yourself I won't get involved, but then these people might draw you in. Then what do you do? Who do you tell your troubles to?

When I saw these fellows, why should I lie, I hesitated a bit, as though my pace had slowed down by itself. It occurred to me this way: they've got to be soused to have a dogfight at this hour of the morning. Now when I'm walking by, they might just leave each other alone and turn on me. If they ended up scuffling like this, remember that the tribe of drunks is given to cruelty as well.

Two men, together, how they threw another against the pavement! They kept pulling him up and letting him go. And the man on the ground had given up, wasn't putting up any struggle at all. That's how I saw it from a distance. I said to myself, Ali, to be brave is not to walk head on into trouble but to manage to steer clear of it...

When he slowed down his pace, Ali felt the cold penetrate his body once again. He took out his hands from his overcoat pockets and blew on them several times one after the other, and then stuck them back in.

...My, my, my, this is not your ordinary cold. But that's all right. Ali, my body, you're on your way to work, not some place else! There're such no-choice situations in life that once you find yourself suddenly plunged into one of them, no amount of will can offset their power. Wasn't it that way in the service too? Once again, today, he remembered his days in the service:

...Well, here I come to military quarters—heck no, no military quarters but some training encampment for raw conscripts—to submit. Still wearing my civvies. Right then and there they make us fall in two by two, put a corporal in charge, and make us march right, march left. How are we supposed to know how to march? The guys behind me, their feet tangle with mine, and mine with those of the guys in front. And that brutal corporal, the more we tangle the more he kicks us with those big combat boots, wherever, catch as catch can. There, you see, there you're in a no-choice situation: you can't escape if you try; you must bear it. You're a conscript.

Was this all then? No, first they took us to the barber—some barbering. A soldier has plopped down a chair before one of the barracks, you kneel before him in line, the guy's got a pair of rusty old clippers, jerking it this way and that, shaving your head, half pulling out your hair. I won't forget the tears rolling down my cheeks. Then, that cruel corporal still breathing down our necks, we march again two by two. Heading for the bathhouse, they said.

When I say bathhouse now, don't you go imagine a regular bathhouse; this is a strange place. The floor is spread cement slab, no windows, and the room a wee bit warm, with I think, two basins. As for us, we're naked as the day we were born; they've taken away all our clothes, including underwear, the civvies being no good any more. We're embarrassed, trying to cover our private parts with our hands. Several seasoned soldiers and corporals, and maybe a sergeant among them, each with a pail of ice-cold water, they begin to splash us. As the cold water pelts our skins we scamper, then huddle again.

Anyway, we got wet; this was the bath episode. We left the bathhouse, and they made us put on these "militaries," which were, for some, several sizes smaller and for others, several sizes larger. Us conscripts had all come out in one pattern, freaky looking in our ill-fitting uniforms...

As he thought this, Ali felt as if sweat ran down his back, despite the cold.

...Now, what if a no-choice situation like some funnel or whirlpool drags me in? There you are, punching and slugging away. Worse yet, what if the police get into it? Right, then how're you going to get out of the mess? Would the police worry about who's guilty and who's not? You're a "tourist," so when they tell you to hand over your passport, what's going to happen? It's all over then.

Keep a hold on yourself, keep a hold on yourself! Don't I keep saying to myself you're here on guard duty over your own purse, don't I? So, why not turn around? But there I was right close to it all. And then both of them took to their heels so fast, not even getting a chance to ride the cycle, that they weren't even looking back. I said to myself, now c'mon Ali, go forth: *Bismillahirah-manirahim*, get going.

And what did I see when I got closer? A helpless old man lying on the ground, maybe in his seventies. He stared at my face a way I tell you I'll never forget, wherever I am. Some gratitude in his look, some gratitude hard to describe. The snot under his nostrils, the tears in the corners of his eyes were frozen like dried chickpeas. His cap was dashed in the snow nearby. His head, ears, back, were all covered with snow. I held his hands; they felt like ice. And there was this dog next to him, like it's on the verge of tears. The leash was tangled around the man's legs, so neither could move. I tried to take him in my arms and pick him up. He was moaning bitterly, and it was a desperate moaning for life, true moans of pain and fright. He was surely in agony.

Then he began to make signs to mean something like, let go, let go. Meanwhile he kept on wheezing. First I didn't get it, then I sort of thought he was saying "the police," and then I got it, that's what it was. "Nix police," I said. "I'll help you, but nix police, I'll get you up and you go home."

I looked up and saw people begin to gather around me. I figured the man hoped for help from the police, but he wasn't thinking of me. And then all these day shift people, they began to say "police" and stuff. That's when I came to my senses. Ali, I said, take to your heels, the situation is getting shitty. I left the man right there and took off, running like anything, turned the corner, and still ran. I heard police whistles. I kept running...

Ali Itir does not know how far he ran. What he does know is that he stopped running only when he reached the factory where he was to work that day. In the dark, the plant was all lit up. Those coming to begin the day shift kept calling to Ali, reminding him half jokingly that it was still early, time enough before starting work. And some were plainly teasing him, even if he did not grasp exactly what they said. When he passed through the gate,

53

the illuminated clock in the plant check-station said precisely eight minutes to six.

Chapter 7

And later, when Frau Gramke left the flat for work around six, a small group of people still remained at the end of the street. They were arguing about what had happened, holding forth with explanations, and excoriating aliens. But Frau Gramke, when she went out the door, did she look in that direction and notice them? If you ask her now, she'll say she doesn't quite remember.

Chapter 8

Brigitte looked at her watch with large Roman numerals and plastic white band; it wasn't even seven. At first glance, she looked determined, yes, but the tautness of her face, the sparkles emitted from the depths of her eyes had vanished; only the restlessness inside her stayed, hardly visible. As she dressed hurriedly, the one thought in her mind was to leave as quickly as possible. But at this hour all the stores and cafes were closed. What would she do if she left now? Especially since she was going to skip work today... That childish stubbornness of hers, that habit of doing right away whatever comes to her mind first, of saying the first thing she thinks of, well, it doesn't always cut ice. Sometimes, if rarely, she also knows how to be sedate, calm, and assured of herself. She suddenly decided that going out now made no sense.

And now, for no particular reason, she remembered the story of the day she and her father were going to the zoo. She hadn't started elementary school yet, she was in kindergarten. She couldn't remember whether it was the supervising girl at the kindergarten or one of the children, but someone had said that on sunny weekends the zoo was so exciting, so full of adventure. You could ride ponies, have pictures taken cuddling tiny lion cubs, sit before the monkey cage and watch their antics, and so on.

In those days, when she returned from kindergarten she used to beg her parents to take her to the zoo like other kids' parents did. She also remembers that her mother routinely put her off. And when begging and waiting for a propitious time weren't worth a straw, there were weeping and stubborn goings on and on—until in fact she got a thrashing from her father.

In those days her sister was everything to her. How often Brigitte had imagined the two of them living happily at a place and time where her mother and father did not exist! Her sister apparently felt the same, because when she was not indulged by them the way she expected, she'd run crying into the kitchen, hug Brigitte and keep crying. Then one day, for whatever reason, neither her mother nor her father could stand Brigitte's pleas, and they promised to take her to the zoo the next day.

She does not remember how she made it to morning that night, but she can still remember fully what dreams she had, and all those gentle, cuddly animals she was with in her dreams. When morning came, though, it was all over. One of those quarrels that never ceased to go away had again appeared out of nowhere, for no reason. As she kept slapping Brigitte's face, her mother swore and screamed. Then Brigitte's crying again, and how the neighbor across the street came to their door, how her father grabbed her by the hand and dashed out into the street; how, huffing and snorting all along, muttering, tugging on Brigitte, who'd retreated into herself in utter dread, and having walked the streets for a time like this, he said, "*All right*, I'll *take* you to the zoo," but then two blocks later, how he ran into a friend of his and they went to the corner tavern instead. And all afternoon how, instead of playing with the lion cubs in the zoo, she played with a huge German shepherd at the tavern and how, about evening, she returned home with her father dead drunk.

So Brigitte can never forget that day either. And when they returned, how she told, embroidering the story, her mother and sister about the zoo. She even told, for days, her playmates at kindergarten her memories of the zoo. All she told came from what she'd heard from them before. She had so appropriated these stories that she'd blended and completed them down to the smallest details in her imagination, making up brand new ones for herself to tell. Her listeners could not quite tell if they were genuine or not.

In the kitchen, without any prompting, Brigitte felt distressed again. And now the cause was perhaps her being unable to stand her ground against her parents, having to accept the things she did not like, wishing to be different and not being able to, or being unable to conceive of a way of being different. If she forced herself a bit more, to sense that she was about to turn a corner would be enough to confound her whole being—even without knowing what scenes lay hidden around the corner.

Everything was in its proper place in the kitchen: the white formica covered cupboard, four chairs with plaid cushions in one corner, the dining table, the gas stove, the lampcover finger-thick in grease, the mirror above the sink, beneath that the cantaloupe-color, imitation-ceramic shelf. On it, two red and yellow plastic glasses, in the glasses toothbrushes and toothpaste, and next to these her father's safety razor, shaving brush and cream, his small bottle of 4711 cologne. To one side of all this three towels hanging, the slightly bowed door to the small pantry space, another mirror attached to the door by a nail; beneath that a checkered dishtowel; then the single pane window of the kitchen and on it the flower-like patterns of frost, which with the heat inside were now quite thawed and drippy.

No time for disarray this morning. The cold coffee's to be poured out and fresh coffee made. The bread, liverwurst, salami, butter, the jam jar haphazardly placed on the table will be relieved of their disorder and tastefully arranged. First she must spread out a table cloth. Next to the coffee cups the bread boards, and next to them the paper napkins.

Brigitte put water on to boil, replaced the paper filter in the coffee cone. All is in place now. But there's yet another precaution to be taken: she anxiously opened her handbag and took out her small purse, and from it the hundred marks she'd swiped from the sugar container, clutching it in her palm, hesitating for a moment, wondering what she should do with it. That's it, she'll put it in her compact. You never know, her father might all of a sudden decide to go through her bag.

She glanced one more time at the carefully laid out breakfast table and gave it a final go-over with an appraising eye. If only there were a flower on it too… No, better without. If there were one, who knows what might occur to her father. The coffee water was about to boil; she could now start cooking the eggs.

"What, you haven't left for work yet?"

Her father stood in the kitchen doorway, in his unpressed, tube like trousers, his grey, three-buttoned, long-sleeve undershirt.

59

Although he knew Brigitte left for work at quarter of eight every morning, whenever he got up, regardless of the time, if she'd not left, he always asked the same question. Brigitte did not respond.

She has no desire to have an argument this morning. She simply wants to sit down warmly, affectionately, considerately at this table she has painstakingly set, just as in those scenes of happy families in margarine ads on television. She wants to sit and savor her coffee calmly and quietly, breakfast peacefully.

"Eggs not ready yet, shall I pour your coffee?"

Bruno Gramke slumped in a chair indifferently, drew the coffee cup toward him impatiently, and puckering his face, pushed away the jam jar with the back of his hand. The happy scene of the breakfast was slowly fading.

"Do you want your egg soft or hard boiled? If you like, why don't you first have a pickled cuke first, good for the digestion."

These last words were for Bruno Gramke a sign, the start of something. He got up, like a ship that would not return to any harbor ever again, staggered over to the refrigerator, took out a bottle of beer, sat back at the table, and bent over the crossword puzzle in the TV magazine.

The breakfast scene carefully placed in its frame was now erased; the frame was now empty.

Chapter 9

The hardest time at the job is between six-thirty and eight-thirty a.m. The cleaning starts with the offices: first the general manager's office, then the sales manager's, and then the personnel manager's. As you go down floors, the work gets heavier; besides, these three rooms need the least cleaning. What makes real work around here are two large offices, one leading to the other: in one, five salespeople; in the other, four people in personnel. And these minxes, they foul up the place so much that every morning you'd think it hasn't been cleaned for weeks, that no one has lifted a finger to clean it. Coffee stains, ashtrays, paperbaskets filled to the brim. Inside them everything you don't need for a day's work: empty nail polish bottles, used paper tissue, cake remnants and crumbs, well, you name it.

And are they smart alecks, these people! If they haven't slept well the night before, if they are champing at the bit, the first people they chew out are the janitors. Without fail they find something wrong, especially something that'll justify their outbursts: the desk hasn't been wiped properly, or the file folders have been moved, things like that... So, there you are, getting bawled out. All right, let's not touch a thing, leave the folders as they are, the letter opener, the pen holder, the paper tray. Well then, how do you clean the desk? How do you dust it when a speck or two of dust so easily irritates these people?

A few days ago, I won't ever forget, I emptied an ashtray belonging to this guy whose hair looks like it's glued to his skull.

He'd stuck his gum in it, left pear stems and cores, cigarette butts piled chock-full, the ashes soaking wet like mud and stuck on the ashtray. You get it, a real pleasant sight. I took it to the sink to wash it out, then something came up and I forgot to bring it back. You should've heard this brimstone. What was it? What if I had broken it, it wasn't any old ashtray, it was a memento, it was this, it was that. I ran to the toilet and brought it back. Here, I said. After all, it could've been broken and believe me the guy would've kept at it until he had me fired. In his pinstripe suite, his glistering gold chain on his wrist, he thinks he's the manager himself. That's why he keeps carping about everyone's work, whereas he's only got the most years in the office, that's all. Does the manager act like that? No sir, even if by chance he finds something wrong in our work, he never lets on. When we happen to meet, he knows how to show he cares.

Where did Hatçe sneak away now? This Turkish woman, she manages to get stuck some place in the most inopportune time, right in the middle of a job. Wish she'd come back before these pain-in-the-neck office workers arrive. Won't be half an hour before the secretaries start turning up. I wish she'd appear now so we can finish up this place. She can hardly pick up her butt, but she's a hard worker; she'll do anything I say. But she can't think of doing anything on her own; you've got to show her what she has to do. She won't say a word, won't balk at all, so I prefer her to a thousand Germans. She's been working I don't know how many months here now, and she still hasn't learned what to go on to when she's finished one job. She'll come and ask me, I'll show her, then she'll go do it. "This is what you'll do," I'll say, and she'll say, "All right, Frau Gramke," and do what she's told. Sometimes I get upset, like why can't this woman think of doing anything on her own. In a way it's better to have her around; even if I snap at her, she doesn't take offense. We get along fine on this; she does pretty much what I say. But where in the world is she stuck now, if I only knew. I'd told her to change the water in the pail, she went and disappeared.

Frau Gramke turned the drying mop over reluctantly and began to mop under the desks.

When the offices are done we'll start on the hallway. When that's about done, it's around five to eight or so, and the secretaries begin to turn up. So now you have them around underfoot. They all wait their turns in the small passageway, where the sink and the water heater are, to make coffee. By nine-thirty the store itself's cleaned: we dust the furniture in the display windows, run the vacuum cleaner once through, and straighten up the piles of small brochures on the counters. The early morning shoppers are always understanding when it comes to janitors. They never disturb us. And once we clean up the sink and the toilets, the day's work's done.

Hatçe was still not around. Frau Gramke set the mop against the wall, crossed the hallway. She found Hatçe hunched over the one corner of the toilet.

"What's wrong Hatçe?"

"Nix," she said, wearily. She was pale; her eyeballs protruded in pain. She was grasping her stomach with both her hands.

"*Ich* a little *schlecht* ," she murmured.

"Rest a bit, you'll be just fine in a little while," said Frau Gramke in a half pitying tone, and emptied the soiled water in the pail, refilled it, then fixed her eyes on Hatçe again.

The sight of Hatçe with her dry, bony fingers grasping her stomach, her eyes rolling in pain, reminded her of Hilde when she was pulled out of the rubble.

...Yes, I think her name was Hilde, always used to wrap a soiled, colorful scarf tightly around her head. She wore a man's jacket, dusty, dark olive-green, and wooden clogs... The crew boss was ruthless; the scurvy bastard never winked if anyone stopped to catch breath. He picked on Hilde; he had no scruples about harassing and hustling her in plain sight of everyone. The occupation forces had stuck an armband on him and in the dearth of men he'd become a crew boss.

It wasn't clear what he'd done during the war itself; only, after the war he'd turned into a super democrat. Whenever he felt like it, he used to chew out all the women in the crew, stretching himself to his full height, imagining he was doing something which took some special skill, putting on airs, too. Couldn't he, seeing one of us trying to move a huge girder or beam or whatever all by herself, come over and give a hand? But no, he wouldn't, because his job was to watch out for dawdlers. Still, this bastard was, for all the women, the man of their dreams. With every excuse to ask him something, they worked their way to him, wiggling their hips. What they asked wouldn't amount to a hill of beans. Like, shall we pile the broken bricks next to the whole ones or some other place? I never played the game. He had his eye on me too. For God knows how many days he kept me in his sight as if he were assigned to watch only me work. Hmmph, I am not about to consider this a chance to sidle up to you like the others, Mr. Crew Boss, I said to myself, you'll see you can't have me.

When a half-wrecked wall, a wonder it still stood, suddenly collapsed, we scattered like partridges, hopping and stumbling over brick piles, running for our lives. We left a trail of wooden clogs and tattered shoes with half soles which slipped off our feet here and there, behind us. After the first wave of panic, we looked at each other quietly, counting. Hilde was under the rubble; we saw her after the dust cloud lifted. We ran over to help her, the crew boss standing over us like a sergeant, giving orders but not lifting a finger himself. You could smell lime dust all around. When we pulled her out, she was half-conscious and kept saying in a pained voice, "I'm okay." It wasn't easy to clear up rubble from seven to five for seventy-two pfennigs per hour and a second-class food ration card with which you could barely get three ounces of phoney coffee, a pound of sugar, and two pounds of meat per month, but no one would want to lose the job.

After the war, you could see signs hanging all around: "Construction workers needed to help pick bricks from rubble." She and Hilde too had hustled over like all the other women in the neighborhood. Who was left in the neighborhood besides women anyway? Except for this mean faced s.o.b.?

Hilde kept saying "I'm okay," but that was what she said. Her wounds were fresh, she was warm, but once she began to cool off, it'd be fine if she could ever get up on her feet, let alone work. When we had the poor woman out, I'd figured it out already, she wouldn't recover fully, that is if she lived through it in the first place...

Hearing an aborted scream, Frau Gramke came to. Hatçe had tried to get up and collapsed again in the same place, hunched over. Then all her face muscles strained, she grunted in convulsions, and then seemed to get over it for a while. Her lips had turned blue, she was trembling top to toe, her teeth chattered.

"Hatçe, what's happened to you? Let me call a doctor..."

"No, no, Ich a little schlecht..."

She said nothing else. When she was up on her feet with Frau Gramke's help, blood oozed down the hems of her baggy pants. Her head was spinning too. But the fact that everything around her spinned slowly as well brought her a pleasant feeling; a trickle all the way from her belly to her heels eased her pain.

Fray Gramke was in a frenzy. She felt she had to do something. In the end, the only thing that she could think of was the first thing she'd thought—calling a doctor.

"Hatçe, hold on, let me call you a doctor."

Hatçe kept shaking her head. Her dizziness blended everything: fears, accusations, self-blame, all mingled together.

Of course your head'll spin and your knees give way, no account woman! Did you have to spread your legs again for that guy you call your husband? Good, serves you right, you dumb woman. You've got four kids already, and perhaps as many abortions, haven't you learned yet?

Each time she blamed herself, she felt relieved by a sense of revenge.

Now you'll go to a doctor, he'll write you down "krank," and they'll give you your walking papers here. This is Germany, what the shit will you do with four kids, tell me you foolish Hatçe woman? What will you do without money, and being a nobody besides? Here you've got a hunkydory job, and how long do you work at it anyway? Add it up any which way it's no more than four hours in the morning, after that you go home. And then, four in the afternoon you go clean newly finished buildings, and that takes about three hours. What else can you want?

The work here is easier; for one thing you don't do jobs by yourself: Frau Gramke watches out for you, the work isn't much, the place's warm. The other place isn't like this, is it? A host of Turkish women, every one of them backbiting, and are they blessed with the gift of gab! And the things they yak about: getting pregnant, having an abortion, how German women use ready-made sanitary napkins.

There's nothing they don't know. You want to know which bank has the best terms for a loan to buy a far field back home, or what's cheap at Bilka, or which firm offers overtime work? Who's taken whom for a lover? They talk about all these, and without any shame to boot. That's all right, you have a job in Germany? Then you're somebody. Even that husband of yours, you see how he treats you, and the more marks you bring in the more you have some power over him. True, he's taken for a concubine that balding German woman he lives with, but he could've taken off and never come around, and then you'd be nowhere with four kids on your hands, couldn't do a thing by yourself. Well, Hatçe woman, doesn't your husband need you more now that you're working, huh? See if you can say no to this, see if you can deny it.

You can't deny it, see, you can't. What can't these marks change? Look, they've even changed your man. Let him pour his maleness into that barren German woman, you just keep on working, at least you're still esteemed back home in the village. But no, Hatçe you willful pig, you just had to go spread your legs for him... Serves you right, so now reap what you've sown, foolish Hatçe, now you'll get your comeuppance once the doctor writes you down "krank"...

"Nix doctor, Frau Gramke, a bit *warten* and it'll go away. It'll go away in no time, nix doctor though..."

For how many days you've been tampering in there with broom twigs. Finally you've made it happen.

"Let me just rest a bit, it'll go away. Nix doctor Frau Gramke."

Ignore it, Hatçe. There, you've gotten over it now. This was easy too.

Remember your first pregnancy? To make sure you had an easy delivery, you went to the jinn conjurer, about morning prayer time, after your bath, ablution, and prayer of repentance...

I sat on a *yashmak* spread on the floor. I blushed, being nervous and abashed. The *hodja* recited and blew on my face, then walked seven times around me. He asked me my name, age, checked out my horoscope. Saying, "O compassionate God," he blew three times. I could feel his warm, heavy breath and my stomach rising. On

68

three days the hodja walked around, recited, blew. Then he gave me a square amulet wrapped in oilcloth, and cautioned me to wear it on days I wasn't clean. If I stayed unclean for over seven hours without wearing it, the amulet would lose its effect, and so he warned me firmly on that. I gave birth to my first child when I was out on the roof laying out noodles to dry.

The female accountant who was the first office worker to come in that morning, when she saw Hatçe in the state she was, put her hand on her mouth and gave out a scream, ran to the phone and dialed 112. Faced with this quick and decisive action on the part of the accountant, Frau Gramke, who had been indecisively standing by Hatçe, felt indescribably depressed.

Chapter 10

That morning, as usual, Brigitte left the house at ten-to-eight. The eaves and roof-top antennas hung with icicles. The blizzard had stopped. Snow looked like fluffed cotton piles on the ground. Fresh tracks of a vehicle or two had left dirty brown lines in the midst of the white. The buildings were endlessly calm, the chimneys among the roofs still sleepy under their white caps. Sidewalks in front of some of the buildings had been cleared.

Across the street, by the main gate of Markthalle, there were two small delivery trucks. A beer truck pulled up behind them. Its engine still on, as Brigitte walked by, the driver briskly lowered the window and said: "How's it going sweetie, it's a cold one, isn't it?"

Despite their apparent nonsense, his words were pleasing to Brigitte. She smiled inwardly, broadly. Whether the driver noticed this smile is not known, but it was obvious that he was emboldened by the absence of a rebuff. He opened the door, and with a showy and agile move, hopped out. He kept speaking, while he opened the sliding side door, his head turned to face her. Brigitte walked on.

...There was in me that morning an eagerness, a passion to begin eagerly everything over again. In some deep place inside me it was as if broad-winged birds were on the wing. Always when I come to the end of our street, I turn left into Lausitzer Square, at the corner of that place whose doors are open night and day, but in which, from the outside, you can't see any sign of life, before whose doors you now and then come across only a drunk or two trying to get in, and on whose black window it says "Sex Bar" in parrot green. That morning, I didn't. I didn't turn into the square.

Where Pückler Street intersects with Waldamer Street, the red-brick building with its stacked roofs, which appears right ahead, attracted my attention for the first time. This difference of roof from other buildings around, the flagpole extending out from the middle window of the second floor, the official importance this pole gave to the building, why should I lie, I'd never noticed before. I was discovering for the first time details around me I was used to living with without noticing.

There was a puny tree in front of the building and someone had thrown a handful of millet around it, where wet pigeons bolted the grain down. If you walked toward them, some took off with reluctant half-wing beats. Others, definitely the more serene, instead of trying to take off, settled for walking away from the tree swiftly and expeditiously. Then they must've figured that danger was not too likely, because they returned timidly to bolt down the grain.

The snow and the cold seemed to have drowned all sounds. I felt like lobbing snowballs on the cars crawling along to avoid getting stuck. Even if I only felt like doing so, this overwhelmed me with a childlike delight.

Mariannen Square looked more unattractive and desolate than it was and bigger. Across the square, the old Bethany Hospital, with its door flanked by two conical towers, looked more like a garrison or a Wilhelmian boarding school than a hospital.

71

Recently, there'd been frequent demonstrations here. There were red spray painted slogans on the walls: *Bethanien muss Kinderpoliklinik werden... SPD lügt... Vorwärts mit der KPD!* The letters, in the solitariness of the place, looked humble and orphaned. Further on, still on another wall another phrase. Try as she might, Brigitte could not quite figure it out: *Fa-fa-şiiz-me...* "And this must be from Turks," she thought to herself. Any more, whatever was alien, looked alien, had to do with the Turks.

On Adalbert Street, the Turkish grocers had opened their stores long ago. Some carried the fruit and vegetable crates they'd brought by car, and some stared out from inside the store, their faces behind the glass panes on the door. It was not clear whether they were looking out for their first customers or merely taking in the scene.

As she passed the cafe where she usually met her friends, she saw it was closed, but the tobacconist next door was going full-steam ahead. For almost twenty years tobacconist Schmittchen had regularly opened up his store at six-thirty every morning, never missing his earlybird customers. And for almost twenty years the store had not changed a whit inside or outside. Out by the door, a long defunct cigarette machine with Richtiger Tabak Geschmack written on it, and underneath that a large picture of a pack of Overstolz cigarettes. Next to the machine three glazed signs, spotted with rust. On one it said, Mach mal Pause; on the next, in gothic letters, Schultheiss Bier, and the third was an ad: Citro-Orange Fürsten Limonade. And the display window something else altogether: a whole bunch of pallid Gelbe Rose cigarillo boxes with a

Melitta coffee poster in their midst. Inside of the store was destitute: on shelves blackened by soot a few cigar boxes, cigarette packs, mint candy, bonbons, packs of chewing gum. Spread on the counter were the Berlin dailies and TV magazines.

When Brigitte entered the store Schmittchen the tobacconist was chatting with a customer about current politics and the events that had lately transpired on the street. For a while they continued their talk. Finally, the tobacconist noticed Brigitte and asked what she wanted. Brigitte laid a ten pfennig piece on the counter, picked up a *Berliner Zeitung* and left. As she went out, the tobacconist and his customer picked up the conversation where they left off, absorbed once again in their chat.

When Brigitte got to the U-Bahn stop at Kottbusser Gate, the train was just arriving. For some reason, she didn't take it, nor the next one, nor the one after.

...I don't know why, maybe it was still too early. I was afraid that if I got on the U-Bahn I'd go to work out of habit. I might lose my battle against routine. So I lingered around the stop, didn't get on the trains that came, and waited for the starting time for work to pass. So that I wouldn't go back on my decision—like waiting for the bridge to blow up behind me so there wouldn't be any turning back. When it was past nine, the first customers must have arrived at red-haired Frau Lieselotte's beauty parlor where I work—her face, eyes, eyebrows painted to the hilt. Yes, I'd managed to miss the starting time. It seemed to me like it was incredible, but I was determined not to go to work and, so there, I wasn't going, I would not go. I'd passed the first test in defeating my habitual self.

73

I took the next U-Bahn. While I was lighting a cigarette, a middle-aged woman stared at me insistently, and I pulled myself in a bit where I sat and gathered the hem of my coat...

After the Gleisdreieck stop the U-Bahn's nose first tilted up, and when at top speed it began to glide down toward the tunnel, an old man sat down next to her, shoving against her somewhat. At the Kurfürsten Boulevard stop, where she normally got off for work, Brigitte fought against herself again, over getting off and not getting off, but did not stir from her seat. She stayed on until the last stop, Ruhleben, still unable decide what she was going to do. She milled about Ruhleben for a while. For a moment she thought of taking the bus toward Spandau but changed her mind. The sunlight resembled glass.

Wandering around aimlessly, she happened to see a public toilet and went in, not because she had to, but to make up her face. She put on dark cherry lipstick, biting her lower lip, carefully making sure she did not get it much past the edges of her upper lip. She rouged her cheeks up toward her temples a bit, drew a light line on her lower eyelid, applied some eyeshadow to darken her upper eyelids, carefully wiped off the excess with a little spit on her handkerchief. When she looked at herself in the mirror, she was brimming with all sorts of mixed feelings... She could not, try as she might, get rid of that childlike look in her eyes, and Frau Lieselotte never left the eye of her mind.

She took the U-Bahn back, getting off the Bahnhof Zoological Garden, and walked toward Kudamm. She had never lived this hour on this street. Mail and parcel deliverers, advertisers, insurance representatives, small-goods manufacturers, distraint officers, display-window arrangers, and who knows how many others of what professions, shuttled in and out of stores. And those who, a briefcase or folder in hand, walked in merely to take a look, seemed more like people on some job rather than customers. And then the tourist groups who certainly would walk through the Reichstag Building got out of their buses and walked in droves to the nearby cafe. Near the edge of the sidewalks the fluorescent orange-clad street cleaners shoveled onto trucks the snow piled up by the slow-moving snow shovel ahead of them.

Brigitte ambled down the boulevard, looking at the cheap jewelry sold on portable stands by hawkers, the decorations in shop windows for the approaching Christmas holidays, and the various advertising signs which goaded people on to spend. Sometimes, she'd linger a while looking at the posters at the entrance to a moviehouse, losing herself in them, instantly exchanging places in her imagination with a woman getting out of Jean-Paul Belmondo's sports convertible or one sitting in her flowing evening gown, next to Terence Hill, at a bar.

Whatever caught her eye, a porcelain plate, a book by an author she'd never heard of, an Italian-looking waiter setting places at the empty tables of a restaurant, she now experienced all this by herself, with no other's eye or words to mediate, savoring it fully. Not that she didn't also think of visiting the zoo, on her own desire and will, independent of anyone, without having to beg someone for it... Yes, she could go to the zoo.

Using an entryway as shelter, she lit a cigarette. She felt cold, turned back, began to walk toward the "ruined church," and entered a cafe that seemed likable enough. She sat on the edge of a chair at a table in the solarium at the front. The electric heaters in the ceiling were all blasting away, but after she got used to the warmth that first greeted her face, she found it was still cold by the glass. She changed tables and chose one a few rows back.

The place was almost empty. She ordered tea, took out the paper from her handbag, and opened it up. On the front page, a headline loud in large type said: *35 Tote bei der Entführung einer Lufthansa-Maschine. Das Blutbad. Auf dem Flughafen von Rom schossen Araber plötzlich in die Menge.* On the second and third pages the rest of the story and several pictures from the scene. *Die Frau des Piloten unter den Opfern des Anschlags.*

They've all gone crazy. Why? What for? Suddenly, she felt a terror she could not comprehend. The feeling awakened a deep rancor mixed with curiosity. The rancor remained; it was a feeling she could identify with.

Sie schiessen, sie schiessen, sie haben noch zwei getötet! She read the news and the captions first with interest, which gradually waned. Soon she began to turn the pages over indifferently:

Spanische Navel-Orangen HK1.II, Tragetasche 4 kg. Füllgewicht 3,98. Schweineschnitzel, frisch, 500 g. 5,48. Lachsfleisch, mager, 100 g. 1,98...70er Beaujolais, samtiger roter Burgunder, 0,7 Ltr. Flasche 3,75...Ungarische Kaninchen bratfertig, gefr. 500 g. 2,98.

She took a sip from her tea and continued to turn over the pages aimlessly.

Bald schuldet die DDR der Bundesrepublik 750 Millionen... Sie brauchen Geld? Kommen Sie doch gleich zur Bank. Möbel+Bargeld bis 20.000 DM noch heute... Grossbankier Deutschlands: Machte er pleite?

When about halfway through, her eye caught the daily horoscope. She looked up Gemini and read with full devotion: *Es wäre gut, auch die dunkleren Seiten einer guten Sache einmal gründlich auszuleuchten. Sie ersparen sich unangenehme Überraschungen.* At first the words bothered her, but then she went round and round in her mind until she believed they verified her situation and spiritual condition. She felt as if all the words were written just for her.

The waitress came by needlessly and, standing over her, asked her to pay for the tea. Brigitte hid her displeasure and ordered another. As the waitress left her, still somewhat sourly, she turned the page to the classifieds where she found what she was looking for. She took two drags from her cigarette, one after the other, snuffed it out in the ashtray, and lit another. Looking like she was dealing with an important matter, she began to comb through the ads under *Sex-Show-Club-Messe:*

Live echte Lesbos shows. Klassische Wunschmassage. Strenge Massage mit Erfahrung. Neueröffnung-neues Team massiert, rassig-mollig-zart-natur-streng. Eberstr. 10, ab 20 Uhr.

Images flashed on and off with lightning speed in her mind: Her sister whom both her mother and father dangled before her at every opportunity as a model for her in life... Who everyone thought was a hairstylist, but in truth was a whore... That big guy, the counterfeit brother-in-law whom they take to be her fiancé, in truth her pimp... On Saturdays, supposedly over to visit and have coffee, but in truth trying to impress them with their new car... Her sister's freshly sprayed, platinum blonde hair... Their handing her father fifty marks to spend for Christmas... The place where she's apprenticed, the red-haired Frau Lieselotte's shop named "Frisör Schnalke"...

She had to try hard to restrain the laughter brimming over inside her. There seemed to be no end to the classifieds:

Salon Diamant-Ganzkörpermassage ab 20 DM, nette junge Damen erwarten Sie täglich von 8-20 h, Berlin-Neukölln, Altenbraker Str. 4. Lederdomina Dolly massiert privat. Babsi massiert privat. Süsses Girl massiert privat....

She marked some of the ads with her eyebrow pencil, tore out and folded the part she wanted and put it in her pocket. Without drinking the second cup of tea which she had just been served, she paid and got up to leave.

Chapter 11

If the hour is about eleven a.m., the covered market is hopping. The elderly, always seeming to start picking up their feet two steps behind them, scurry as best they can over to wherever there's a friendly chat at whichever counter. Whether it's because it's only women customers who do the little shopping around noon or what, the male owners of the stores have turned over the counters to their wives, themselves busy with stocking the morning deliveries, vegetable and fruit crates, sacks of bulkfood, and cases of pop and beer, or figuring debits and credits on their orders. Perhaps they've stepped out to down a shot or two at the bar by the entrance to the market. At these hours the market, you might say, belongs to women.

"I said to her, look I said, it just won't work this way! Didn't listen to me. And what happened? What good did she get out of it?"

"Did you say two oranges? How about one of these eight-pound bags for three ninety eight?"

"Well, if she'd listened to me then, she would've paid six hundred and thirty marks; now she has to pay six hundred and eighty..."

"Yeaah, that's true."

"Some potatoes too for me, four pounds... No, I can't carry any more than that."

"Look here, though, the winter's barely here; this much won't last long, will it?"

"It won't, it won't. I bought the cauliflower yesterday at twenty-nine a pound, today it's thirty-one. Besides I've never seen anything get cheaper."

"How many pounds of onions? I don't have any plastic bags, but if you'd like a paper bag..."

"Ten eggs come to two marks and ten pfennigs. Do you have ten pfennigs? Well, all right, if you don't have it, it's okay. You can pay me tomorrow. Good-bye..."

At Schulze the egg vendor's, fat Erna, as soon as she saw Frau Gramke enter the store, had her customer pay and got rid of her. She turned to the poultry woman next to her and in a louder voice said, "What was I saying? Oh yes, you know Ernst Kutte, well, I hear he's finished..."

She cast suggestive sideways glances at Frau Gramke and went on with her story, seemingly indifferent to her: "Schmittchen the tobacconist went to the hospital with him. He told me about it. Looked like it was pretty hopeless. Guess it was a foreigner shoved him down, then was seen running away. He had all sorts of broken bones from the hips down, frozen to boot. He was taken right away to emergency care."

...This half-wit is at it again. A moment ago you were telling the story so loud that I should hear it, but no, that wasn't enough, you're not sure whether I heard or not, you want to know what I'm going to say about that stupid old codger with his dog. That's what you're waiting to hear. Well, lick your chops as long as you want; I came here to shop, not to gossip...

Though she had resolved so many times never to stop by fat Erna's counter so as not to hear all the gossip, not to listen to this woman who could be counted on saying the worst that can happen, she could not help herself. And here she was, when there were plenty of eggs in the refrigerator, needlessly buying more.

"For hours the man lay out in the snow! What's a man that old doing outside? In such weather, and in the pitch dark of morning, too. Walking his dog's only an excuse. What do you say Frau Gramke, am I not right?"

...You're right, you're right, now stop acting so naively. I know you'll keep asking till you find out, I know you. You think I'm going to say, "Yes, Frau Erna, you're right, that old geezer, not heeding his age, makes an excuse of walking his dog morning and night, actually hoping to run into someone he can talk to." Well, today you're knocking at the wrong door...

"I'd like some of those small ones, the sixteen-pfennig ones, I'm making a cake."

"Yes, Frau Gramke. Serves him right, he was a pain in the neck that codger. I hear when he was younger he was a pain and then some, was shifty in those days too. I don't know what he ate, but I sure know he drank beer by the pack. He used to buy it regularly at the market, and nothing else, except maybe a can of peas or a jar of carrots. At least I never saw him do otherwise. Well, to tell the truth, no one else has either, but did you Frau Gramke? After all, he's your neighbor. He'd drink and drink and then go out, and why? Supposedly to walk his dog!"

A whine in Frau Gramke's ears. She paid for the eggs and left. She went through the whole length of the market and came out at Eisenbahn Street. A sleety snow was coming down again. For a instant, in the half-deserted street, she expected Ernst Kutte to appear around the corner with his dog.

...I wasn't ever like the other women. How they kissed up to him at every chance, so he'd wink when they sleazed a bit on the job. They'd even sleep with him for not much more than a couple extra tablespoons of sugar or half an American cigarette. I know he had his eye really on me, but he got zip from me, the mean opportunist. Oh, he was in the civil service, oh, he was actually an important person... What was the difference between an important and an unimportant person in those days? They'd said he'd worked at the armored vehicle production at Daimler-Benz in Marienfeld. Whatever the shit it was he did, he'd managed to stay on his feet, hadn't he, and that was what mattered. Perhaps being a do-nothing, being good for nothing, had made him important then. Sometimes not being at all important could apparently make one important. I don't care who is how important, that shifty guy was of no consequence in my eyes...

The whine in Frau Gramke's ears continued. She still stood by the other entrance to the market as the sleet swirled by the wind blew against her face.

...What was her name, Hilde or something, the woman we dug out of the rubble... One day, she'd run over to us terror-stricken, stood right before us, her hands half in her mouth, frozen in fright. She trembled all over, her eyes popping out of their sockets, but not

82

a word from her lips. She was gasping, trying to catch her breath. Though her body trembled before use, her mind was somewhere else. Later, when she was able to speak, we couldn't figure out what she was talking about. "There," she kept saying, "over there, in the basement." She pointed toward the ruins among which an entryway to a basement still stood, where we now and then went to get warm.

To tell the truth, we'd met up with so many unexpected situations, lived through so many extraordinary events, that we couldn't even imagine what could've startled and terrified her like that. Perhaps it was a pretext for us to quit working and gather around her, asking, "What is it? What happened?"

She'd had to pee and wanted to find a suitable place past the entry, toward the back of the ruins, but suddenly her foot had snagged on something. Just as she began to tell us, she screamed and began to cry again, sobbing. How funny that scream had sounded. The crew boss, Ernst Kutte, sliding down a pile of bricks and rolling down like a ball, had ended up on his feet right over us, scolding everyone, barking: "Stop making a big deal of whatever happened. Are you itching for trouble? Go on, keep working."

There was nothing we could do, so we went back to work, except that some of the women could not refrain from making mocking insinuations about Hilde, giggling as they did so, acting like they were giving the crew boss the eye… I think maybe just one of us remained by Hilde and tried to comfort her.

The event provided the crew a with diversion for the whole day. One after another, the women began going to pee. I held on. I held on and on till, right before quitting, I had to go. I could've gone and squatted down some place else, plenty of ruins around. I suppose everyone's curiosity had rubbed on me too. The entry to the basement was rather wide, more like a room than an entryway. Farther ahead there was a sink that somehow had survived, which we used as a toilet.

It was dark there, and I walked on a bit, feeling my way with my hands. I walked on, rather worried that I too might trip on something. At every step it got darker. I didn't feel like going farther, so I stopped. I'd just begun to gather up my skirt when someone behind me forcefully grabbed my crotch. I was startled. As I was trying to pull myself together, another hand grabbed my left breast. Just when I was trying to figure out what happened, I heard close to my ears the crew boss Ernst Kutte's drooling whispers. I wanted to scream, but I couldn't make a sound. Besides, why should I resist? To resist was a concept that had so lost its meaning... Then, too, I needed a ration card and work. Together we fell over on something soft.

Then, suddenly, some kids appeared in the entrance to this dark corridor. The closest one to us, well, more truly the one with the deepest voice, said to the others that if they were not scared he knew where the corpse of the horse was and he could show it to them. Then one of the kids cried out, "There, I see it, and it's moving too." And all of them ran and scattered like a handful of shrieks. The one with the deep voice kept calling after them, "Hey, you dummies, would a dead horse move? Why're you running away?"...

84

Chapter 12

Frau Gramke has been to this tavern several times, but she's never seen the place like this. To top it all, they're not even drunk, though for them to be drunk by this hour is easy as pie, saying first, let's have a short beer, till one of them orders a round of drinks, and that's it, the spark is lit, then another, then still another, and finally, the bartender fills another round, so there you go, in less than an hour all the noon regulars of the place turn into priests in the pulpit delivering sermons. They all talk at the same time, no one listening to anyone else.

At first glance, what surprises Frau Gramke so much is how crowded Pückler Corner Tavern is at this hour. All the faces belong to acquaintances: Manfred the secondhand store owner, Günther the grocer, a few others from among the other retailers in the market, the construction worker Dieter who's out of work all winter, the coal dealers Treutsches, father and son, and Paul the neighborhood mailman. Each with a glass in hand, they were gathered around a well-dressed man, whom Frau Gramke did not recognize, giving him a hard time. And especially Bruno, who was so ardently pressing him that if the man tried once in a while to get a word in edgewise, Bruno cut in, saying, "Herr Stadtrat..."

When she entered, Frau Gramke had stood for a while before the door, and when, unlike ordinarily, no one paid any attention to her, she'd brushed off the snow on her overcoat and approached the counter. Only the coal dealer Treutsch senior had noticed her coming in, and in a faint voice through toothless gums with a cigar in between, had said *"Guten Tag,"* halfway getting up from his barstool, offering her his seat. When she'd gestured no with her hand, he'd sat back again and resumed listening to Bruno attentively.

At first Frau Gramke tried to make sense of the conversation which seemed to go on as if it had lost half of itself, sliced in the middle. As far as she could make it out, she figured there was perhaps a new proposal concerning the people of Kreuzberg before the city council; every so often somebody came around to take a few soundings.

Bruno Gramke, as if he had read her mind, uttered this bookish sentence: "Herr Stadtrat, you always come and consult with us after you've reached a resolution, and after you have decided to implement it."

Among Bruno's audience rose murmurings of assent. The coal dealer Treutsch senior uttered a "Bravo" without removing his cigar.

"All these talks, all this is a comedy, hypocrisy, right?"

There were more bravos for Bruno. Manfred the secondhand store owner said, "Prost Bruno" and downed his remaining beer. The bartender pointed to Manfred's empty glass with his eyes, as if to say "another beer?" and when Manfred nodded, he filled it halfway.

Bruno Gramke was emboldened. He continued what was perhaps the first earnest settling of accounts with his taciturn self: "On the one hand, you shouted, 'Freedom opens its bosom to you,' at the top of your lungs, so that some of us, when we heard the word 'heaven,' thought it was here, and then, when we left the Soviet-occupied area and came to Berlin, you treated us like fugitives and put us in immigration camps for months. Let's say those were the early fifties, things weren't quite in order yet, but was the aftermath really different?"

When Frau Gramke saw fat Erna the egg vendor enter, she turned away, recoiling.

...This woman saw me enter here, and oh, now she's about to start telling again what happened to Kutte from number sixteen. Let her begin and she'll get what comes to her. Now Bruno, why've you stopped now? Go on with your talk! How close you were to checkmating this Stadtrat fellow! My brave husband, go on, or this chatterbox will start to yak...

Ignoring everyone, Erna stretched her thick neck toward the counter and ordered a cherry brandy in her cracked voice, her cold hands swishing as she rubbed them together, and talking advantage of a momentary silence in the conversation, "They say tomorrow is going to be like this; the radio report says it's going to snow tomorrow too," she said.

The councilman first ordered another beer for himself, then as if he just remembered it, he asked if Bruno would have another. Bruno nodded, and then, whether to save face or the situation, the Stadtrat asked everyone one by one what they would have. While all spoke up at once, some asking for vodka, others for whisky, and still others for beer, only Erna thanked the councilman. She ordered another double cherry brandy.

87

"I'm a tailor by trade," Bruno Gramke began again, not in any shape to notice that Stadtrat was not inclined to continue the conversation. "When I came to Berlin there was no work to speak of. We worked wherever we could find a slot, at whatever job we found. Then reconstruction began and I found a job in my trade, in a garment factory, tailoring women's overcoats. When we bought our first TV set for nine hundred marks at that time, we felt like we'd bought the world, right Greta?"

Frau Gramke, glad she was noticed and considered important enough to be asked her opinion by her husband who was being listened to as he led this conversation, sat up imperiously. With a strange feeling of triumph she looked at Erna the egg vendor because Erna could not now find an occasion to speak of old Kutte.

"... At one point, they transferred me from tailoring to ironing, claiming the work was being rationalized. Piecework ironing anyone can do if he has the strength, and for a few years I did it too. As I got older and began to fall behind, they handed me my parting wages, and they said it was because of the 'energy crisis.' Instead of me they hired the Kümmel Turks. Had they ever seen a factory back in Anatolia? Do they know what rationalizing and whatnot are? Nope, the only thing they know is how sweet the mark is."

"Leave the Turks alone. They're good people," said Manfred the secondhand store man, souring his face and giving a serious air to his voice. But Bruno was all fired up and not about to stop.

"When it comes to words, it's good people, humanity and all that! Democracy, equality, that sort of stuff! Whereas actually it's all a matter of what's in it for whom, right? What I really

88

mean to say is, they didn't live through what I lived through, though I haven't lived their lives either. When they've lived what I lived through, then we'll be equals. We'd even sit across a table over a beer, right Herr Stadtrat? Otherwise, that they've mustaches or that their breaths stink of garlic is of no consequence to me."

A nasty silence in which no one knew what to say followed. Erna the egg vendor, having swigged the last drop of her double cherry brandy and preparing to go, stopped short, and as if she had just thought of it, turned to Frau Gramke: "They phoned Schmittchen the tobacconist not too long ago from the hospital, because he was with Ernst Kutte from number 16 when they took him there. The old man passed away."

As she went out the door, she turned around and added: "His heart just gave out. Maybe it's better this way; he didn't suffer at least. He had no one to look after him..."

She gave Frau Gramke a distant look, as though only Frau Gramke knew the old man, as though none of the others did.

Chapter 13

Ali Itir had spent the morning coffeebreak in the toilet. Because he hadn't had enough sleep the night before, or because he'd half frozen in the cold of dawn, or because he'd shoveled snow in the factory courtyard—whatever. After using the toilet, he sat there, his eyelids drooping, and dozed away. As he dozed, his days working in construction at Beşiktaş began to stir before his eyes.

This was the first job he'd found when he reached Istanbul: the construction of an apartment building with a mosaic tile facade— who knows who lives there now?—right across from the State Wedding Office. All day long couples were married there, one after another. Some of them took place without a crowd, not much joy in these. But then there were the others... Well, well, well... Crowds of people, in private cars, in taxis. Then everyone at the construction site would stop work, mingle with the wedding crowd to get some candy, and even some gratuity from the groom.

When such weddings took place, people who appeared out of nowhere—a host of vagrants, all sorts of beggars, children running in from the nearby neighborhoods, women carrying infants with pacifiers in their mouths—milled about the State Wedding Office.

The parking attendant charged with putting into some order the cars in the narrow little space serving as a parking lot at the bottom of the hill would, for such weddings, give himself an air of importance, and try with greater care than usual to clear the way for the the top-drawer relatives of the bride and groom, whose cars he immediately identified amongst the crowd. Indeed, if he were annoyed enough, he would, with the dictatorial sharpness of a police officer, scold and scatter the crowd of spongers whom he knew to be uninvited, and so restore public order in his own way. Then, straightening the navy blue, visored cap which he thought gave him an air of officialness, he'd toady to the groom's family to wangle a big tip in return for his services.

If he were satisfied with the tip, his authority was then absolutely beyond challenge; he'd really get tough right and left, and quash and quell all those uninvited, whom he could identify because they were not dressed up. But if he thought the tip too little, he would slip away and leave the teeming and jostling crowd to itself. And on those occasions when wedding pictures were taken before the building, leaning against his pick, Ali had, many a time, wistfully imaged himself in place of the groom with his neatly trimmed and dressed hair, his dark suit, embracing the bride with her flowing bridal veil.

On his morning break, nodding in the toilet and sweetly recalling these images, Ali had been startled by an irate knocking on the door. After he pulled up his pants, he'd come out, splashed a little water on his face, and stuck a cigarette in his mouth. Then, having smoked only less than half of it, he'd gone back to work. This time, they had brought him inside to work in the basement warehouse.

It seemed as if noon would never come. When it did, and he and the Meister directing his work in the basement went up to the cafeteria, it was crowded. His stomach cramped with hunger. The smell of food in the cafeteria made him ravenous. Two olives were all he had eaten all morning. Ah, if only he could now have some meat stew cooked with plenty of onions and some tomatoes!

The Meister hadn't gotten in line because he'd brought his lunch, and so he'd sat down at a table right away. When Ali got in line, he thought everyone was staring at him. He felt intimidated. There wasn't a single familiar face around him—a nasty situation he recently found himself in more and more frequently. For a moment he didn't know what to do; he felt as if on all sides his body took up too much space. He rubbed his eyebrows, then his mustache, with his fingers, then stuck his left hand in his pocket, but he still felt uneasy. He took out his small string of prayer beads and fingered them nervously.

"They sport a personality, that's what they do when they go to Germany and come back," Haydar had said to him in a coffee-house at Tophane. "Why else would anyone go there? You'll earn marks, you'll sport a personality!"

Well, Ali had decided to go to Germany, and the fact that he'd been declared unfit at the State Employment Office hadn't fazed him either. "Decided" is hardly the word. He'd gotten his passport and his train ticket long ago. His friend Haydar didn't yet know his resoluteness and loved to make know-all statements: "This Germany business, it's screwed up everything, I swear everything. Let alone those who go and return, if you stay behind, your 'personality' too is measured against those in Germany. How can anyone here keep up with those in a mighty place like Germany?" And Ali had ascribed these laments of Haydar to his also being declared unfit, and so his envy of those who could go.

The woman doling out the food extended the bowl of pea and sausage soup and asked Ali for his meal ticket. Darn it, what ticket? He just started work today; he had no "meal ticket" and stuff. He stared vacantly at the woman's face. She wasn't a bit polite to him and repeated her question condescendingly: "I said meal ticket, don't you get it? People are waiting behind you."

Weeell, you can see I don't have one, so why keep insisting? If it's a matter of paying, I'll pay, whatever it is!

The woman shook her bewildered head side to side, as if to say, "What in blazes, how could anyone get in line and get food here without a meal ticket?"

Ali had taken out a handful of change from his pocket and was saying, "*Wieviel? Wieviel?*" and extending it to the woman.

Now she was even more peevish.

"*Nix Geld, Marke,*" she said, rebukingly.

Just when she was withdrawing the proffered bowl of soup, someone behind Ali handed him a ticket. Before he had a chance to turn around to see who it was, the words he heard came to his rescue: "It's all right, brother, welcome. Was it today you started work?"

Ali had not, understandably, expected this. Now it was his turn to be befuddled. It was the student or whatever he was, the gabby young man from last night.

"I've been working here for two weeks. I'm going to work a month longer, and then the semester starts," said the young man as he seated himself on the edge of chair at a table. "We stayed rather late at Bücür's tavern last night. I almost didn't get up on time this morning. But all in all, it was good. Our friends are all alert people; we had a good talk."

How should Ali respond now? Should he say, "You talked, yes, and what good did it do? Did you get rid of the label 'illegal alien'?" He said nothing. If he had to confess the truth, he wasn't altogether unhappy that he came across the young fellow here. But when he thought the fellow would soon loosen up his tongue, he was worried. "Good thing you showed up, else the woman wasn't about to give me any food," he said, at least to have said something.

"Enjoy it."

"Thank you."

He spooned up his soup. He was certainly hungry but he didn't hurry; he took his time eating. The longer the meal was the less time for a talk, or rather, for the the young fellow to talk and Ali to listen to all the confusing stuff. When at last he finished his meal, he wiped his mustache with the back of his hand, lit a cigarette, and used the other end of the matchstick as a toothpick for a while. Just to fill the silence he asked when the lunch break would end. "One o'clock sharp," the young fellow said.

The cafeteria clock showed there were still four minutes to one. For an instant Ali thought he might find a suitable moment to ask if there were any hope for illegal alien workers. Ever since he'd heard of the police hunting illegal workers with dogs he was frequently dispirited. If he could only solve this problem, if he could only shake off this illegalness thing, he'd show that woman Sultan and that jackass Ibrahim. He'd show them first, how someone becomes a "personality" in Germany. If he could just be freed from his dependence on them, they'd see what a person Ali Itir would be...

"Well, so it goes," the young fellow said. "I was very glad to see how sharp those friends were last night. You know, brother Ali, we didn't come here just to buy shirts, radios, tape players, or cars. When we leave we're going to have a new personhood in our suitcases too."

...There, you see, he even knows my name. Must've been Halim, the big mouth. What time is it now, not yet one? Would this lunch break end! Now look here, Ali, you must be a hopeless case, why would anyone want a break to end? Aren't you the one whose bones ache with fatigue? Let the man talk if he wants to talk. If you don't want to listen, you just pretend you're listening and that's the end of it. My, my, Ali, seems you've got no smarts at all. You see, this is Germany, there's all kinds here, and this man here's one kind. Wonder if I should ask if there's any news about illegal aliens? Whoa, you jackass Ali, ask, go ahead and ask and ask for trouble! You'll see, at quitting time he'll wait for you, take you over to that meeting place again. Then you'll have to sit there and listen to words you can't make any sense of, like "...and this individuality, this personhood will be our new consciousness when we return to Turkey."

What had Haydar said at the coffeehouse in Tophane? "This Germany thing, it screwed up everything. Whoever goes and comes back from there acts like a somebody." Well, if you listen to these educated types, Haydar is right. Return to Turkey and try to act

95

like a somebody only to be disgraced before Haydar? Would Ali Itir ever return? No sir. By hook or crook, he'd manage to stay here. Hadn't he gotten here that way too? And if he's going to sport a personality and all, he'd do it here, or the sort he'd sport here would not pass in Turkey...

Ali was quite pleased with these thoughts.

...If I could only rid myself of this fugitive name and stay here, if I could only nullify this "tourist" stamp in my passport by another stamp! Now Haydar, you were so right. Take this student fellow, even he thinks of putting some personality in his suitcase and returning. So of course you're right. This Germany thing, it sure screwed up everything. Who you are is measured against those in Germany, even if you're not one of those who came here and went back, and it begins with the watch on your wrist. Now, how could you compete against the personality this guy brings from Germany? Of course you're right to be upset, Haydar, right as can be. I will stay here...

Ali was happy that he'd now set his desire to stay on such a solid foundation, but at the same time, when a host of questions which he couldn't understand, couldn't resolve, couldn't find even a routine answer to came to his mind, he frowned. What if they try to do a major search with police dogs in Berlin too? What if they sniff out Ali and find Ibrahim's place? My God, let Ali be a somebody, take away those dogs from Ali's trail! Hey, if I could understand what dogs speak, I'd tell them my troubles too, even throw them a huge bone, he thought.

The bell signaling the end of lunch break rang. Ali and the young fellow snuffed out their cigarettes and stood up, and the student said as he was leaving, "Let's get together again for lunch tomorrow. In the morning, though, don't forget to go by the personnel office to get meal tickets."

Ali nodded, and he instantly felt a bitterness: would he be working here tomorrow too?

Chapter 14

Who would've thought it would happen? Frau Gramke does not remember feeling so restless at home in the afternoon. Here she sits, for almost an hour now, chain smoking. She made some goulash but didn't at all feel like eating anything. She looks around her vacantly. Bruno isn't back yet. He's stuck back in the beerhall with the councilman. Likely he's drunk now, no point in going there.

Twenty minutes to three, she couldn't stand it any longer. She left the house quickly and stopped by the tobacconist at the corner. Schmittchen wasn't there, but his wife was, and two customers Frau Gramke didn't recognize.

She reached over to the TV magazines piled on the counter and took one out, randomly turning the pages. Predatory birds nearly extinct in their natural habitats in Germany. On the corner of the page, in a square frame, there was a photo of an eagle amongst jagged rocks, about to take off. Her eyes were on the photograph, but her mind wasn't with it; it was lost in thought, and the print on the page was effaced. From the back of the store, the Schmittchens' living room, a clock struck a muffled three. The two customers she hadn't recognized had left. The tobacconist's wife asked her if she could help her. As Frau Gramke quietly closed the magazine and placed it back on the pile, their eyes met for an instant. All through her, Frau Gramke felt those ineffably complex feelings of estrangement that people who are caught red-handed feel.

"Guess you heard it," said the tobacconist's wife, as if she were passing on a secret. "My husband just left for his apartment to gather up his papers; on the way to hospital he gave him the key to it."

"So it is true, Thank you. Goodbye."

Frau Gramke crossed the street and ran straight toward Pückler Street, number 16. When she reached the second floor landing, she stopped for a moment to catch her breath, gasping. She climbed the stairs slowly to the fourth floor, pressed the button under the brass-alloy plate engraved with E. KUTTE in gothic letters. First a silence, then the patter of footsteps inside; the tobacconist opened the door. From the way he stared deeply into Frau Gramke's eyes, clearly he was surprised. He pushed back the hair on his forehead, running his fingers through it.

"Ah, it's you," he said, "I wondered who it might be..."

Another feeling of uneasiness in Frau Gramke now. This time she felt through and through that she was someone not expected. In utter confusion, she hesitantly asked if she could do something to help. Perhaps she could help tidy up things.

The tobacconist asked her to please come in. As they walked through the orange wallpapered hallway, he felt, for whatever reason, the need to offer an explanation.

"Not clear how it happened. Witnesses say someone pushed him. In fact, they insist it was a foreigner who ran away from the scene," he said. "His hip was broken in so many places. According to the doctors, he actually died of cardiac arrest. Apparently he'd begun to freeze, having been out in the cold for so long... Though they saw the man who pushed him run and called the police immediately... So it must not've been too long a time..."

That same whine in Frau Gramke's ears again. Like the deep whine of a machine in freezing crisp air, which the cold cannot engulf and stamp out, a whine heard from very far, piercing the ear without losing volume, nor letting up—a ceaseless whine.

They walked into the single room of the hallway. Frau Gramke, in a voice like a sigh, managed to say, "Please let me know if there's anything I can do," and collapsed into an armchair with all her weight.

The small room was disordered. The bed had not been made; next to a discarded grey armchair were a low table full of empty bottles and beercans and a plate soiled with dried-out potato peels and leftover food. The carpet was torn here and there, exposing the wooden flooring underneath. Before the tile-glazed stove, newspapers were spread, on which the ashes from the stove had been emptied in a heap.

The apartment had not been maintained for years; it was dirty and smelled of old clothes. Frau Gramke, hunched over in the chair, was considering whether to start tidying up. No, she was thinking of nothing. There was only the whine in her ears. Her eyes caught two framed, yellow photographs on the wall behind the TV set. One was of Ernst Kutte as a medic before a field hospital sometime around the First World War. On the mat framing the snapshot was a quatrain written in a neat hand:

Die Artillerie zu Fuss und Pferd
Ist stets des höchsten Ruhmes wert

Sie spricht ihr Wort mit dem Geschütz

Das klingt wie Donner, trifft wie Blitz

and underneath, a note:

Zur Erinnerung an meine Dienstzeit.

without a date.

In the second photo, the whole crew of rubble clearing women posed before the ruins. Right in the middle was Ernst Kutte, in his late forties, his right arm turned at the elbow toward the camera so that his crew boss armband is clearly visible. Next to him, smiling diffidently, an arm over the shoulders of a woman in a military jacket, herself, Greta Herbolzheimer, her name in those days.

The tobacconist sat in a chair by the window, going through a folder with various papers, documents, and insurance vouchers in it. He'd forgotten about Frau Gramke.

"I better be going now, my husband's waiting for me at the tavern," she said, suddenly getting up. "If I could help in some way... Actually that's all I came to say..."

The tobacconist said that he too would have to leave now, for he had to report the death to the funeral affairs division of the registry. He placed the folder in a plastic bag, and putting on his coat he said: "He'd taken out insurance for his funeral. Always said to me, if I die you let them know. So he wouldn't be a burden to anybody. I'll leave all his papers at the police station..." and stepped aside to let Frau Gramke go out first.

Chapter 15

It was a weird place. That woman, wearing only teeny lace panties and a pair of patent leather boots up to her knees, sitting half-reclined on that sofa with tassled, velvet throw pillows, how she used the situation to her advantage, how stuck-up she was; you'd think the sun rose and set on her. And then the way she took a drag from her cigarette, the way she moved her heavily mascaraed eyelids with cheap eyelashes from Woolworth's, reaching over now and then to the table next to the couch to take a ceremonious sip from her drink, ostentatiously tapping off the lengthening ash on her cigarette on the ashtray... You'd think she was posing for a *Playboy* centerfold; cut out this picture and hang it like a poster on a wall. And then her rising and putting on the record player Chantilly Lace singing Sha-na-na, shutting her eyes while humming along, confident that she'd given her face the liveliest and sexiest of expressions, swaying her body as she stood there... No doubt she thought herself an irresistible, raving beauty.

How she made me feel small, as if I had just come in from a playground. Conceited bitch. The one who opened the door was more sincere. What was it the other said? I should come back when I grew up some; customers don't like to see children. With breasts like small fists, how would a man want me? And her? What about her own sagging things?... She's envious, that's all. The devil said, take her poses in those patent leather boots and tear them to pieces, fling them away.

The other, the one who opened the door, was at least telling the truth. She said she was afraid of their getting into trouble with the police. That was okay, a way of explaining... And I could've said, don't worry, I'm not at all as young as I look and so on, but I couldn't think of these then. I said nothing. Something had stuck in my throat. True, I did not see, after she closed the door on my face, how the two of them sat together and burst out in laughter, but I heard it. Whatever happened, it was a crappy place, anyway.

As she descended the stairs, Brigitte felt both nauseated and relieved. The light fixtures on the walls, the ruffled curtains, those patent leather boots, that woman sitting half reclined on the couch—all revolved in her head, mingling with the singing of Chantilly Lace, and the pain of having been humiliated weighed on her with all its might. She felt the devastating power of not having been able to save herself from the humiliation. What did you have to do to be grown up? The question engulfed and shook her whole being, forcing her to seek an answer which could deliver her from her present helplessness.

For a moment she viewed herself on the two full-length, plaster-mold framed mirrors facing each other at the ground-floor landing. She stuck out her tongue at her image playfully. The marble handrail curving down by the stairs like the neck of a swan nestling its head under a wing was also reflected in the mirrors. At its end there was a large sculptured lion's head. She imagined herself in a scene from the movie *Sissy*. When she walked out on Ranke Street, she joined the flowing crowd and reached

Wittenberg Square. Suddenly she remembered Achim. And with that, Achim's motorcycle brought her back to the world she knew.

The sleet came down intermittently. In the beams of headlights butterflies of snow swirled playfully. When Brigitte arrived at the cafe where she usually met her friends, Frank and Alfred had settled down at the farthest table by the slot machine. She asked if Achim had come by.

"Well, we're here, aren't we?" said Alfred, pointing to Frank, and drank up his Coke, then belched deeply.

Frank pulled a chair for Brigitte.

"He's not here yet, but he'll be here soon," he said. "Why don't you have a seat?" He sounded persuasive.

This guy has a sensitive side. He's quick to grasp things, and in the least likely circumstance tries to rescue whatever needs to be rescued. There's warmth even in his constant kidding. He was like that now: "Last night he didn't have anyone to curl up with, so he hopped in the sack with his cycle. He was so satisfied they couldn't separate the two. Shall we go get him up?"

Brigitte forced a smile.

Alfred shook his head. "The old geezer was all curled up, lying there in the snow, about to freeze..." he said, trying to pick up the story where he had left off before Brigitte came. Frank ignored him altogether, and, raising his thin nose, he sniffed the air deeply.

"Phew! It stinks here, smells rotten," he said.

All three at once looked at the doorway. A policeman waiting for his curry sausage ignored them as if he had heard nothing of what was said.

Chapter 16

A little before quitting time, Ali had shyly approached the old Meister he worked for that afternoon and managed to ask in his broken German if he were to work there the next day. His heart kept pounding as he waited for the answer, and he kept silently repeating "bismillahirahmanirahim," begging God to help him out... C'mon now, old man, just say "Yeah," be good to Ali, huh?

The Meister acted as if he were ignoring him, but it was obvious he was evaluating Ali's work for the day. What did it matter to him? If it weren't Ali, it would be someone else. There's the snow to be shoveled off the courtyard, and the factory is moving to another place, so the stuff in the warehouse has to be reviewed, separating the old supplies no longer being used, crating replacement parts for products no longer on the market to be sent to the main warehouse. And the Turk didn't work too badly, to tell the truth; he did everything asked of him without saying a word. Hadn't he seen all kinds among these one-day-at-a-time workers? Drunks, thiefs, pigheaded ones, goofoffs... The personnel people had said, if this guy works out, you can tell him to come back for a day or two again, hadn't they?

"You be here at six a.m. again tomorrow. First, you'll shovel the courtyard, then you'll come work for me," said the Meister in an indifferent voice. Then, a bit more friendly, he added, "Well, how did you like the work?"

...I'd like to kiss your lips for saying that old man! May your lips never have to tell troubles, old man. Liking is hardly the word. Let there be work, no matter what kind. Hey, will Ali let you do anything at all yourself? Tomorrow and the next, day, and the day after you just sit there in your corner, you sweet little old man, I'll do your work too...

"*Ja, ja, arbeit gut*; very *gut* too," Ali said, gesturing with his hands to indicate the work was fine.

After quitting work, on his way to the office where he'd left his passport that morning, if he weren't embarassed by it, forgetting the snow, the winter, the cold, he'd dance with joy in the middle of the street. Every part of him sang a different tune—his feet, his hands, arms. Who gives a hoot about the cold? He doesn't even feel it!

...My, my, my, come down blessed snow, come down for six months, a year! You come down so that Ali, your subject, will have work. If you wish, never stop, come down forever...

At the office there were a few others besides him. Except for one, they all looked German. The man behind the desk in the morning was paying off one of them. He looked at Ali standing there before him out of the corner of his eye. Ali grinned. If he had the means, if he could speak some German he'd certainly have said some thankful words to this man too. After all, he was the one who'd found him the job. But the man was nothing like the affectionate man he was in the morning. He nodded toward a chair and told Ali rather brusquely to sit and wait for his turn.

...Why get upset, brother? Right, I'll wait, no problem. It's my fault. The guy's busy, and I just walk up there and stand over his head. Why couldn't I have thought to sit first?...

He sat down in a chair. The man called one of them, asked him when he started and when he quit, then worked out some figures, and after paying him, called another. Ali had made exactly twenty-six marks and twenty-eight pfennigs that day. The man first gave him two ten-mark bills from the safe, then the rest in change, and returned his passport.

Ali had already been working out some figures in his head: If I work for ten days, I'll make two hundred and sixty marks, twenty days and I'll make five hundred and twenty marks... O my God, you've finally seen to Ali in his distress! Let Sultan and that jackass Ibrahim turn green with envy now... Well, well, well, Ali is full of himself now.

The snow kept coming down. When he walked out, he pulled up the collar of his coat and took the shortest way to Bilka. At the Kottbusser Gate intersection, in the confusion of the evening traffic, zigzagging between cars lined up waiting for the light to turn green, he tried to lose no time. When he reached the store, his feet knew where he was headed: the men's clothes department in the back. He almost ran, bumping into people right and left. There were only a few customers there; the loudspeaker played tender Christmas tunes, which delighted him.

He stopped before a row of dark suits, checking out the prices. Most were between a-hundred-and-thirty and a-hundred-and-fifty marks. He took a striped suit from its hanger and held it up at arm's length, trying to image how it would look on him. If he could put on this suite and arrive at their apartment dressed to kill, what would Sultan and Ibrahim have to say?

He glanced at the price tag and began to figure out how many days he would have to work to make a-hundred-and-thirty marks and ninety-eight pfennigs. If he made twenty-five marks a day, six work days would be enough. When he figured out that at most in six days or so he could buy such a suit he was elated. In a matter of six days' work he would take the first step toward being a big success as a personality. "Is it Ali you're talking about?" they would say, "O, Ali is one huge personality. Just look at that suit on him! Anyone wearing a suit like that has got to be a somebody."

He dreamed like this until the saleswoman came by and asked him if she could help. Uncomprehending, he shook his head to mean no. He handed the suit on its hanger to the woman, and ignoring what she said behind his back, he hurried to the shirt counter, from there to socks and underwear, then to the sweaters.

...Now this sweater is not bad. It's nice and thick and good looking too! And it's twenty-eight marks, I could buy this tomorrow, for instance. And the shirts are twelve marks and fifty pfennigs. I could buy one now, but no hurry with them...

Finally he thought of his wet socks, and he bought a pair from among the cheapest, on sale for the day for 1.80. As the store closed Ali was the last customer to leave.

He put his hands in his overcoat pockets and clutched the small package of socks tightly in his palm.

Chapter 17

Brigitte paid for her Coke. She didn't pay much attention to Frank extending her the Bacardi bottle on her way out, saying, "Come, take a swig, it's cold out there."

She shook her head and said, "*Tchüss.*" She was nervous, didn't have the assurance and liveliness she had in the morning. She'd hoped to have seen Achim. She had to talk to him, explain why she had to go home early last night. If need be, she was going to apologize. She had an endless longing to lean against him. She wanted Achim to be next to her now, but despite all her desire, she could not get near him. On the contrary, she felt clearly she was moving away from him. Even the lines of Achim's face were receding in her imagination and then were being erased. Only his tattoos remained; they were there plainly in sight.

This was a rupture and Brigitte lived it with all its tremors. The house she lived in two blocks ahead was now was fading away, being erased, and the streets she walked seemed like streets she did not know or recognize. Faces were different, sounds were different, lines were different. They all were being transformed. She felt as if the bags of onions, the hanging garlic, the walnuts, tangerines, bananas, apples in the steamed up window of the grocery store she was going by were things whose names she had never known. Perhaps all this was a dream, a play, or a movie.

And just as in the movies, she walked toward two men whose backs were turned, who faced the glass door of the beer tavern in the corner, trying to make out some people inside.

"Got a cigarette?"

The man was startled and turned around to face her.

Brigitte repeated, "You got a cigarette?"

Ali Itir didn't know what happened to him. He used to hear about, didn't he, in bars and so on, interesting meetings with women and incredible stories of such meetings, but nothing like that had so far happened to him. He looked down, avoiding Brigitte's look. "*Jaa*, cigarette, of course," he said.

Ali is now in a swing: one push and they're having their pictures taken before the wedding office in Beşiktaş, and he's the groom in the navy blue suit, embracing the bride. Another push, and swoosh, he's the unwanted guest in Berlin, at the home of Sultan with the big butt and Ibrahim the jackass. Another push still, and the scene shifts: he's a worker in a factory, stacking spare parts in the warehouse. And yet another push, and he is where he is now: a young woman before him, his head spinning, and he trembling all over in excitement.

...Ali my boy, this is another day altogether. It was clear it would be this way even in the morning. Fortune keeps coming to your door today. What should I say to her? If I offered, would she come and have a beer? Halil the blabbermouth always says: German women you invite to have either a beer or an Asbach-cola with you... We'll go to Bücür's tavern, it's a place I know.

There you are Ali: you've got money in your pocket too, and tomorrow's work is in the bag, at least you won't be embarrassed. Dammit, how do you say it in German? If I say *"Zusammen Bier,"* she'll probably understand...

Fumbling, he took out and extended the cigarette pack to her.

Must light it too. Matches! No, not matches, I have a lighter don't I? But which pocket is it in? Damn luck, I think it's in my pants pocket. Let me undo my coat buttons.

Brigitte had drawn very close to him as Ali tried to light her cigarette. The lighter in his cupped palms kept going out in the wind.

"Scheisse! The damn thing, it's wet already."

Brigitte angrily flung the cigarette on the sidewalk. All the German words Ali knew bounced up and down in his mind, but he could not grab hold of any of them.

"*Scheisswetter, wa?*"

"Weather *nix Scheiss, nix Scheiss!*"

What else can he say? If only a few words rolled off the tip of his tongue, if only he knew how to speak German, like that student fellow.

...Why don't you talk, you son of a bitch! How can he talk? Were he to tell the truth, he would not be spared the beating anyway. It had happened once, during military drills, when they were given a rest period. Those who had to pee had gone over to a bushy slope behind the drill area and done their thing. Ali too had gone. Then he saw a few soldiers behind a bush who'd gotten hold of a donkey which they were trying to hump. The one behind the animal was in such ecstasy that he moaned away: "That's it, now bump and grind, oh pretty girl, oh kohl-tinged eyes!"...

After months without women at the barracks, the others were on the verge of shooting off just standing there and watching. In this situation, Ali hadn't been able to desist either and had queued up behind the others for his turn. Then, what was done was done. Those who'd managed to flee had fled, but Ali was seized by the sergeant with the two stripes. "Hey, you tell the truth you son-of-a-bitch, did you do it or not?" The sergeant slapped him, his hand smacking Ali's face on the way up and down. But Ali was mum. Not a word escaped his lips.

"*Schön Frau, du kommen Asbach-Cola trinken?*"

He felt relaxed now. He'd managed to rattle off a sentence of the kind worthy of that student fellow, he thought.

"Don't you have a place? Best we go there, but it'll be twenty marks, okay?"

Ali almost said, "*Nix*, no *Haus*, I'm staying with Sultan and Ibrahim, relatives." Again he could not put the words together. He nodded.

Together they walked toward Admiral Street. Brigitte noticed as if for the first time that the building at the entrance to the street was being razed. The other buildings had also been evacuated, their windows boarded across and their entrances bricked up.

They stopped in front of one. The center panel of the main door had come off and been replaced with masonite. The dim light from the entrance reached the inner courtyard and half lit it—a courtyard like a pit. They walked on to the right wing of the building. It was shabby and rundown all over. A sharp odor of urine lingered in the courtyard.

Ali pressed the button for the automatic hall-light. On a cast iron door there was a rusty, tin sign with *Zur Tischlerei* in faded

113

painted letters on it. The plaster on the walls in the stairs' landing was cracked, the linoleum on the stairs thoroughly worn out.

Again, as if she were in a movie, Brigitte followed him half curious and half shuddering. They walked up to the second floor. When he unlocked the door, he hesitated: should he enter first or should he show the way to the lady? What if she changed her mind? His heart pounded as if it would burst out of his chest.

He doesn't know which one of them came to the rescue by giving way, but there the two were inside already, the corridor-like area whose one end was used as a kitchen, and the other, where he had his bedding. The odor of scorched fat and onions mixed with the smell of drying clothes on a line stretched between two walls. Brigitte now suddenly sensed she was beginning to feel sick at the odor, the sight of this place, this room, and Ali standing there forlorn, like some captive. And he sensed that he must get over his hesitancy, say and do a thing or two. When he saw Brigitte's sour look, he dashed into Sultan and Ibrahim's room and turned on the light, inviting Brigitte.

"Bier trinken? Ah, nix Bier, Tee trinken?"

She didn't respond. If this business has to get done, let's get it over with, she thought. Once begun, it's easy to finish. Come, get this thing done! I want to get out of here as soon as I can...

Her gaze panned the room. There was a bed by the tile-glazed stove. On the bed was a bedspread of shiny pink material, and at the head of the bed was a huge plastic doll in a wedding gown. The doll's eyes were shut. By the window there stood something resembling a china cabinet, showcasing a mess of trinkets: gilt-edged demitasse cups, a bottle of eau de cologne still in its cardboard box, a coffee-table cigarette lighter, several framed photos, a rather large beer glass with the Berlin coat of arms with bears in it. About the middle of the room there was a kitchen table and four chairs; on some nails on the wall hung clothes wrapped in newspapers.

He asked again, "Nix bier trinken?"

She ignored him again, and suddenly she decided to walk over to the bed and began to undress. She took off her overcoat, her sweater, and everything else she had on one by one and threw them on the floor, gazing intently at him.

The swing in his mind returned and it went back and forth so fast that he could not make out a single image: everything swung back and forth. The only thing that stood still in his mind was the thought: would this girl change her mind about this business and leave?

He tried not to look at her nakedness but could not overcome the compulsion to glance out of the corner of his eye. Just to have something to do, he too took off his overcoat, and bent over to untie his shoelaces slowly. When he took off his shoes, he felt embarrassed with all his being about his wet socks with holes through which his big toes stuck out. As if he were covering up some shame or guilt, his back turned against her, and trying not to face her at all, he picked up his coat and shoes and slipped into the kitchen.

For a moment he didn't know what to do. He sat on his bed, took off his old socks and put on the ones he had bought. When he returned to the room, she stood before the bed with her firm, pink-nippled breasts, her bellybutton, the blonde hair on her genitals, stark-naked. Now, Ali cannot be held back. No one can stop his aroused virility. Almost beside himself, he went to work on her with all his might, grasping her on the shoulders on both sides of her neck with his hands, trying to push and shove her down on the bed.

Brigitte, not quite understanding what was going on, found herself in inexorable panic. She wanted to scream, to break loose and be free. The panting face pressing against her covered her mouth and nostrils, and she could not breathe properly.

For one moment Ali straightened up and quickly slipped off his trousers. He was struggling to stick his erect member into her but couldn't manage it. Her body was frozen stiff all over, and she squeezed her legs together with all her might. He had to make do with holding fast to her. His fingernails were sunk in her shoulders. He came and came in spasms... When he calmed down, Brigitte tried to sit up.

"Nix fertik, nix Geld geben, nix fertik," Ali said in a voice like a moan.

The panic she felt began to grow again in large and terrifying whirlpools, swallowing up the most private nooks remaining in her. She wanted to run and be free right then, from this bed, from this doll in the wedding gown at the head of the bed, from these odors of scorched fat, onions, and drying clothes lingering everywhere, from those coffee cups in the cabinet, the bottle of eau de cologne in its box, and most urgently, from this creature pressing on her like a nightmare, who or what he was she didn't know, not even his name.

"Nix fertik, nix geben, schön Frau."

As Ali tried to stroke her face, Brigitte began to cry "Help! Police!" at the top of her voice. As soon as he heard the word "Police," Ali roughly covered Brigitte's mouth with his large hand.

"Nix screaming! Nix police, *bitte!*"

These last words were said as if on the verge of crying, in a childlike voice, something like imploring. Brigitte felt a yielding ease; she thought it was all over. Ali was docile now, lying on his back, his hands covering his genitals, staring at the ceiling. A silence had settled in the room. The things that went by before Brigitte's eyes: mounted on round-rumped horses ambling in unison, heavy armored medieval cavalry, all with faces she recognized, holding in their hands various instruments for cruelty and torture— all sorts of whips, spits, vises, pincers, and cauldrons of scalding oil to be dripped, drop by drop, on the most sensitive parts of the body...

In the silent room the crackling of wooden furniture could be heard. With a sudden retumescence Ali began to force her again. Another scream from her... She felt as if she were in the bottom of a dry cistern, hearing her scream echo in her ears. She felt ineffably frightened and alone.

Brigitte does not know exactly how she freed herself from this nightmare. The only thing she knows is that she tried to put her coat on while descending the stairs, madly, two steps at a time.

Chapter 18

Yes, she'd said so: approximately an hour ago she met a stranger. The stranger, taking advantage of the darkness and the solitariness of the place, forced her to go to his apartment and assaulted her, threatening her verbally and physically. The event has taken place without her consent and with the use of force. Not content with this, the assailant has also taken a certain amount of money from the girl's purse. Her looks, which suggest exhaustion from fear, and her agitated recounting of the event indicate that she's still under the effect of what she's gone through. One can plainly see signs of shock. Her disheveled state, eyes which prove she has wept, the mascara running down the sides of her face, the fingernail marks on the shoulders next to her neck, all show certainly something has happened to her. That the assailant used force is undoubtedly the case.

He'd weighed over and over what he'd been told and evaluated the situation as he saw fit. The deputy chief at precinct station #107 sensed that an assault might have taken place. What he doubted was the credibility of her account, especially the hour the event would've taken place. The bad weather and the darkness could've been contributing factors, but it was hard to believe that someone resisting, struggling, and crying for help in the middle of Kreuzberg around seven in the evening could be dragged by force all the way to an apartment behind a courtyard.

The deputy chief read aloud the statement he pulled out the typewriter: "...After he forcibly did his thing, he let go of my throat. He began to rifle through my purse. When he was putting the money he found into his pocket, for a moment he must have forgotten about me, so I ran out. He ran after me, but he couldn't catch up."

To the question of whether her statement was accurate, Brigitte said yes by nodding.

"Berlin, 18 December 1973... Would you sign here." The deputy chief compared the signature with the one on her identity card and returned the card to Brigitte.

Later, accompanied by two officers, Brigitte would go back to the alleged place of the event; the officers would investigate the courtyard, the stairs; they would knock on the door to the apartment, but there would be no answer.

After that:

One of the officers would write down the name "Ibrahim Gündogdu," handwritten in crooked letters on a piece of cardboard and stuck on the door with a thumbtack; they'd find the doorkeeper who, worried at seeing the police officers, would tell them that behind the courtyard, in the right wing of the building, old Frau Vezky and the Gündogdu family lived; that they were all registered with the police, that no unregistered persons lived there, not to mention that he, given his job, would not wink at anyone's so living there; that he had seen the Gündogdu couple leave for work that afternoon: that they worked for the most part at night, and that he happened to know the name of the firm they worked for.

119

Following that:

The police would track down in the register the name "Gündogdu," and learn that the couple were Turkish citizens, that they'd been living here since 8.1.1971; then spelling out the name by code—Gustav—Übermut—Nordpol...—ask a squad car to check with the firm at Kanal Street, Berlin 47, to see if they came to work that day and report this to the station immediately.

When the officers arrived at the firm, they'd be told that Sultan Gündogdu and Ibrahim Gündogdu came to work night shift that day right on time, and the officers would, at this cement and asbestos plant, see with their own eyes their time cards rung in at three p.m., and record this fact. Furthermore, Sultan and Ibrahim would be hurriedly brought in to the division manager's glass partitioned office; they would answer in a credible way the questions asked of them, swearing by God that no one lived with them, absolutely, and these statements which sounded convincing would be recorded as well.

Moreover:

On the way back to their work, Sultan would rebuke her husband, saying: "All these months he'd been staying with us! He may be a cousin but being a guest so long is too much. And does it make any sense to run from the police? Nothing more can be done. I wish he hadn't turned out unsuitable and come here properly. And now he'll ruin us too, get us kicked out of Germany." Ibrahim would answer these words with, "Enough of your talk," but inside, finding her right, he'd think, we've done our human duty. It's enough already; if the police are on his tracks, well, he'll have to grab his suitcase and leave, hang by his own leg. Then, turning to his wife, "Whoever asks, we don't know any Ali. He's unknown to us. No one named Ali Itir ever stayed with us. You tuck that in your ear and don't you go saying anything else," he'd instruct her one last time.

As for Brigitte, she'd be taken to be examined by a doctor, the doctor would determine from the bruises and fingernail marks on her shoulders, about her neck, and by other medical means the sexual assault, tell the police that the event could've occurred at most about two hours ago and that he'd send them a written report later. All the details emerging from these statements and the police investigation would be written down, signatures affixed, dates recorded.

However:

Brigitte's restlessness would not diminish. Since there was no suspect being held for the crime, what could she tell her family, how convince them of the event, and how prove that she was telling the truth? As she thought of these, her restlessness would grow even more.

And so:

When she was brought home at around ten at night, accompanied by a female officer who'd narrate the event to the household politely, decorously, and suggest that they should deal with their daughter tolerantly, assure them that the police are searching for the offender and that the event would come to light in all its details in the shortest time possible—all this would be for naught, for after the officer left, her father would give her a sound beating and then, saying, "What the hell did you do with the hundred marks?" beat her once again. And Brigitte would experience once more, with all its bitterness, the fact that after all these official procedures, this movie too, in which she starred, amounted to nothing.

So that:

Despite her story being recorded, she'd not be able to convince anyone close to her of the truth of her account, and the next day, the day after that, and after more days still, when she insistently told the same story, Frank, Alfred, and Achim, all would laugh it off as untrue, except that her father, whenever the subject of money came up, would not be able to restrain himself from reviling her.

Chapter 19

Ali's situation was not at all cheery either. He existed officially in birth records, but he was officially non-existent here, and according to statements made to the police, he was one whose clothes, color of hair, height, weight and so forth were on record, yet a fugitive whose identity was unknown.

After Brigitte left the apartment, he too had dashed out, run to the courtyard, intent to pay her the twenty marks they had agreed on and to mitigate his fault somewhat, but he could not catch up. By the time he was in the courtyard, Brigitte was already on the street. Hesitating about running after her further, fearing the police might soon be around, he'd made up his mind to get away from the building and not to be seen in this neighborhood again.

He'd realized that he was without his overcoat only when he was out on the street and felt the cold, and with all the speed he could muster, he had run back, put on his coat, straightened up the bed as best he could, and just when he was about the go out had noticed the wet socks he'd taken off, had sort of wrapped them in some paper and stuck them in his pocket, and had quietly opened the door and gone out again.

Were his steps shorter than usual or were the streets longer? He does not remember when he comes to the end of a street and how long he has walked up another. He has an ineffable sense of regret; if someone so much as touches him, he'll start weeping. If he hears the slightest stir behind him, he turns back in fear, expects the police, who he imagines are tailing him, to appear from doorways, behind corners or trees, and arrest him. And after a while, when no one appears, he starts walking again. Street after street. And if the street he's now walking is Friesen Street, when he sees, even in the far distance, the lit up Polizei sign, he turns back and heads toward Chamisso Square.

He was certainly running now. It was as if again that tall man were chasing him, when Ali was five or six years old. Wearing a visored cap which made him look older, a hand-me-down coat in which his puny arms disappeared, he was running barefoot. He'd stolen some tomatoes from a vegetable garden and was caught in the act by that very tall man.

"Son, stop, will you! Quite running so haphazardly! Look out, there's a water hole ahead, you'll fall in. Go on, keep the tomatoes. It's all right, stop running!" yelling after him, that very tall "uncle" Aras.

Ali doesn't heed the words, no way! He's running and starting to cry, sniveling. He flings away the tomatoes, head turned back, his eyes fixed on that very tall man, running from the one who caught him redhanded. Before him a deep water hole, a pit full of green sediment...

He hadn't fallen in, but he would never forget how frightened he'd been then.

As the night went on, he felt more disgraceful. Especially as the thought that his dream of doing guard duty for his purse, of becoming a somebody, was fading, slowly vanishing, worked into his consciousness, a peculiar dejection took hold of him, his bitterness grew, and he pitied himself: if he let go, he would cry.

The blizzard had picked up and it had gotten colder.

"Should I go to Bücür's tavern or the place last night? Help, oh my God, help Ali, don't leave him in these straits! If someone came by and said, 'How are things Ali?', how can I answer? I'll blush, come unhinged, and start to stutter, words and body and all, and I'll feel ashamed. What can you do when someone's personhood is trampled so in plain sight? How remedied? Oh my God, why don't you show the way to your subject Ali in this land of misery they call Germany!"

Chapter 20

December 29, 1973. This final Saturday before New Year's Eve, the entrance to the market looks like an anthill. Those who've done their shopping, scurrying out with bags bursting full, those who've not, rushing in. At the liquor store by the entrance, beer, wine, and champagne are being bought not by the bottle but by the case. The baker selling *Pfankuchen* and the fish seller are doing very well; customers have queued up before their shops. A gluttony, a greediness that someone witnessing it for the first time would think it's a time just this side of some huge famine.

On street corners, doorways, firecrackers and cherry bombs are exploding. The New Year's fireworks already set off rise with their insidious hissing as they take off. It seems as if the place is the battlefield for a prosperity being consumed. In this revel of noise, a few young women and men hand out political handbills in the corner of the market. One, a megaphone in hand, ceaselessly repeats in a hoarse voice slogans like

> *Gegen Entlassungsterror und politische Unterdrückung!*
> *Gegen Lohnraub, Arbeitshetze und Teuerung! Deutsche und*
> *ausländische Arbeiter: eine Kampffront!*

Not much heeded by anyone, the voice fades and is lost among the noises of cherry bombs, firecrackers, the whistle and rustle of fireworks.

Frau Gramke entered the tavern at the entrance to the market and began to collect money "as they felt they could spare" from the early regulars. A little while ago, she had gone through all the floors at number 16 Pückler Street, from door to door, trying to collect money for the memorial wreath. Some had gotten rid of her saying they had no change; others, affecting generosity, had handed her a mark or two to be done with it.

She had not collected much. The people in the tavern were more generous, both hand and heart. Whomever she walked up to, they first raised their glasses to "old Kutte," mumbled a kind word or two, and handed her at least a five-mark bill.

When Frau Gramke stopped by the flowershop and ordered a wreath for Thursday, January 3, 1974, the florist first hemmed and hawed, saying the New Year's business was going to be heavy as usual, so he might not get the wreath ready in time. When he finally agreed to the date, Frau Gramke had to select the most appropriate wreath for the price among the samples. The one she selected, excluding the ribbon, cost fifty marks. Another fifteen marks would go for the silk ribbon. And on the white silk ribbon for the wreath for Ernst Kutte, it would say in black letters: "*Unserem lieben Nachbarn einen letzten Gruss.*"

Chapter 21

The man behind the counter in the cafe had cleaned the counter, emptied the showcase, having put away the meatballs, chops, and pickles in the refrigerator long ago. He walked over to the table where Achim, Alfred, Frank, and Brigitte sat, and they paid their bill. Alfred was the first to leave, saying he needed to buy some new straw and woodshavings for his guinea pig. Achim did not have the slightest wish to leave; he could have a beer or two more. He began to tap his fingers nervously on the table.

The man collected their empty glasses, saying, "Well, we'll see you in the new year," politely intimating it was time to leave. Achim stood up. Brigitte had promised to go out with him this weekend, but now she was saying she could not go out tonight. Her sister was to visit; she did not want to disturb the settled calm at home. But Achim was ready to cause trouble again; he insisted on her going out tonight.

"Are you coming with me now?"

His tone was threatening.

"No, I just told you why I couldn't, didn't I?..."

Achim walked out fuming.

"Achtung, Achtung! Hier spricht die Polizei!"

A dark blue police van rolled slowly past the cafe. On its top was a display dummy. Next to the dummy there was a fairly large phantasmic drawing of a face.

Brigitte froze, dumbfounded. She felt something icelike slide down her spine, quick as lightning. The face in the drawing, the overcoat, trousers and shoes on the dummy...

Yes, it was he...

"This was the man, this was the man!" she half cried out, jumped up, and ran after Achim.

"Achtung, Achtung! Hier spricht the Polizei! On December 26, 1973, the person whose face you see in the drawing was found dead in Landwehr Canal, wearing the clothes on the mannequin. He might've committed suicide or been the victim of an accident, or possibly of a murder. Since, despite all investigative efforts, his identity has not been established, the police seek the aid of citizens. Who saw this person in these clothes for the last time and where? In whose company was he? Who is this person? Who can inform us about the acquaintances of this person? Who can supply other information about this event? Information which will help in identifying this person can be reported to any police station. Any statements given will be held, upon demand, confidential."

The voice on the loudspeaker repeated these words in Turkish.

Chief detective Michael Heymann already felt, through trained intuition, that no matter how much they drove around and repeated the message, the police would not uncover any leads. And about two weeks ago, when they discovered three Turkish citizens, two women and a man, murdered on the fourth floor of an apartment, at 25 Naunyn Street, he'd realized for the first time in his career that he'd bumped against the deaf walls of a mode of thinking, feeling, and living to which he was a stranger.

129

The police van slowly rolled out of Adalbert Street, leaving behind the trailing, metallic sound of its loudspeaker.

For a moment, a very brief moment, everything around Brigitte whirled. As they whirled, their shapes dissolved and they were transformed into shapes without any meaning. She gasped frantically and gulped again and again.

Achim, a little ahead, was trying to start his cycle parked on the sidewalk. When he noticed Brigitte suddenly appear next to him, breathlessly saying, "It was that man, the man whose picture they had on the police van," he stared at her face with a vacant and somewhat pitying look and shook his head.

"Oh come now, don't start talking that nonsense again," he said, impassively.

"Achim," said Brigitte, her voice diffident and childlike.

Achim raised his head. "What is it?" he asked.

They gazed at each other silently.

Suddenly Achim asked again, "Are you coming with me now?"

Brigitte looked down, and without a word she climbed on the back seat. In the pale light of noon, Brigitte and Achim, both, how splendid they were.

Notes

Translator's Acknowledgments

I'm grateful to my colleagues James R. Reece and Gerd Steckel for their generous help with the German passages, and to Annes McCann-Baker, the Series editor, for her patience and understanding.

Guide to Turkish Sounds

All Turkish vowels and consonants are sounded. The English word in parenthesis contains an approximately equivalent sound:

a *(son)*
e *(trend)*
ı (the second vowel of *mortal*. The last name of one of the characters is spelled in this text as *Itir;* pronounce both vowels as described here.)
i *(is)*
o *(only)*
ö *(earl)*
u *(push)*
ü (not in English; as in French *tu*)

c *(jell)*
ç *(chop)*
g *(gas)*
ğ (consider unsounded; lengthen preceding vowel; the second *g* in the name *Gündogdu* in this text)
h *(hall)*
j (like the *s* in measure)
r *(rest)*
ş *(shop)*
y *(you)*

Other consonants are similar to their English counterparts.

(**Notes** continued on next page)

Endnotes

Chapter 3

Page 29
An-und Verkauf, We buy and sell.

Chapter 5

Page 42
Scheisse, shit.

Page 46
Lieber im Stehen sterben, ..., Better to die standing than to live on your knees.

Chapter 6

Page 52
Bismillahirahmanirahim, In the name of the merciful and compassionate God. (The opening phrase of each *sura* of the Kur'an, invoked by the faithful in initiating a significant act.)

Chapter 9

Page 64
Ich a little *schlecht,* I a little sick.

Page 68
"krank," ill. (The doctor will certify you're ill and so unable to work.)
a bit *warten,* a bit to wait, i.e., wait a bit.

Chapter 10

Page 72

Bethanien muss Kinderpoliklinik werden... SPD lügt... Vorwärts mit der KPD!, Bethany must become a children's outpatient clinic... The SPD (Social Democratic Party) lies... Forward with the KPD (German Communist Party).
Fa-fa-şiiz-me, fumbling attempt to pronounce the Turkish word *(faşizm)* for fascism.

Page 76

35 Tote bei..., 35 Dead in the Hijacking of a Lufthansa Plane...Bloodbath...Arabs Fire into Crowd at Rome Airport without Warning.
Die Frau..., The Pilot's Wife among the Victims of the Attack.
Sie schiessen...They shoot. They shoot. They've killed another two *Spanische Navel-Orangen...,* Spanish navel oranges, class #2, in a 4kg carrying bag, 3.98 DM; Pork schnitzel, fresh, 500g, 5.48 DM; Lean salmon, 100g 7.98; 1970 Beaujolais, velvety red Burgandy, 7/10 liter, 3.75 DM; Hungarian rabbit, frozen, ready for frying, 500g, 2.98.

Page 77

Bald schuldet die..., Soon the GDR Will Owe the Federal Republic 750 Million...You Need Money? Why not come to the bank right now? Furniture+cash up to 20,000 marks available today...Germany's Most Prominent Banker—Did He Go Broke?
Es wäre gut..., It'd be good for once to illuminate thoroughly the darker sides of a good thing. You'll spare yourself unpleasant surprises.
Sex-Show-Club-Messe..., Sex-Show-Club-Fair, Genuine Lesbian Shows, Live! Classic massage (massage of your desire). Rigorous masseuse with experience. Re-opening. New massage team gives massages: fiery—cozy—delicate—uninhibited—rough. 10 Eber Street, after 8 p.m.

Page 78

Salon Diamant-Ganzkörpermassage..., Diamond Salon—Total body massage, from 20 marks, nice young ladies await you daily from 8 a.m. to 8 p.m., Berlin-Neukölln, 4 Altenbraker Street.

Dominating Dolly gives massages privately. Babsi gives massages privately. Sweet girl gives massages privately.

Chapter 12

Page 85
Stadtrat, city councilman

Page 86
Kreuzberg, district in (West) Berlin, where the largest population of Turks now live.

Page 88
"Kümmel" Turks, from German *Kümmeltürke*, a general term of contempt, now (as here) used ethnically.

Chapter 13

Page 93
Wieviel?: How much?
Nix Geld, Marke, Not money, ticket.

Chapter 14

Page 100
Die Artillerie...
　　The artillery on foot and horseback
　　Always deserves the highest praise
　　It speaks its piece with the cannon
　　Sounds like thunder, strikes like lightning
　　　　　　　In remembrance of my time of service.

Chapter 16

Page 107
Ja, ja..., Yes, yes, work good.

Chapter 17

Page 110
Tchüss, "So long" or "See ya."

Page 111
Zusammen Bier, together beer, i.e., "Let's have a beer together."

Page 112
Scheisswetter, wa?..., "Lousy weather, isn't it? Weather no lousy, no lousy."

Page 113
Schön Frau, du kommen Asbach-Cola trinken? "Pretty lady, you come drink Asbach-Cola?"
Zur Tischlerei To the cabinetmaker.

Page 114
Bier trinken? Ah, nix Bier, Tee trinken? "Drink beer? Ah, not beer, drink tea?"

Page 116
Nix fertik, nix Geld geben, nix fertik, "Not finish, no give money, not finish."

Page 117
Nix screaming! *Nix* police, *bitte* "Not screaming! Not police, please!"

Chapter 20

Page 126
Pfannkuchen, pancakes.
Gegen Entlassungsterror..., Against firing terror and political repression! Against wage robbery, hurried work (pressure to work too fast) and high cost of living! German and foreign workers: a united front in the fight!

135

Page 127
Unserem lieben...., A final farewell to our dear neighbor.

Chapter 21

Page 128
Achtung, Achtung! ..., Attention! Attention! This is the police!